Inside My Mind Volume I

A Collection of Stories

978-0-9880864-9-4

Published by Science Fiction and Fantasy Publications

Inside My Mind Volume I/Douglas Owen – 1st Edition

Summary: Short stories are a fantastic way for an artist to expand their abilities. The short stories in this collection range from 300 – 7,000 words in length. Most were written as exercises to push creativity as well as force minimization of words. The stories represent different genres and styles. First and third person perspectives are used as well as past and present tense.

0 9 8 7 6 5 4 3 2 1

To my wife
I still can’t believe she hasn’t left me

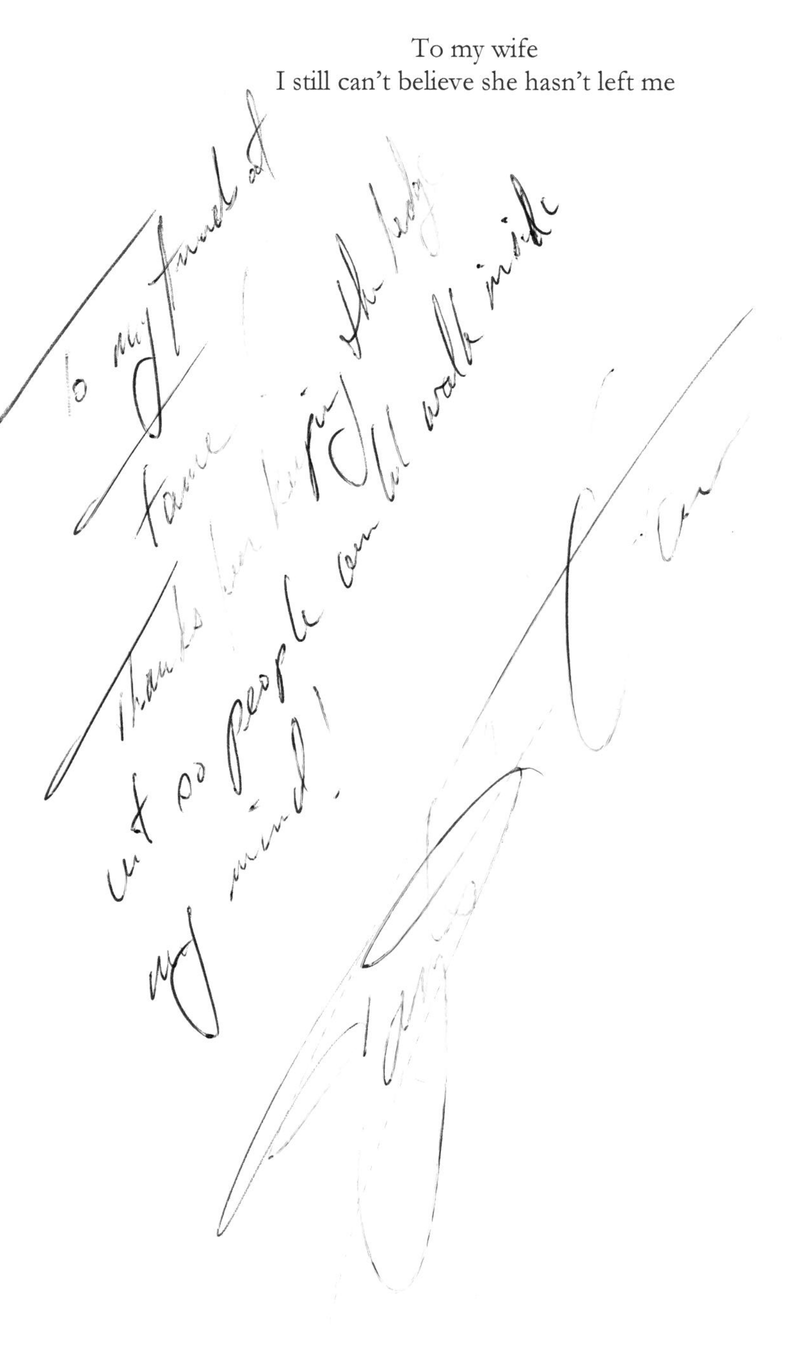

The End of the World

Time of Death

I lie on the bed with my eyes wide open, watching the time on my phone move towards 04:00 hours. For some reason it's hard to sleep. It has been that way for months. Nothing has changed in life, besides the ever present possibility of being called in for work early. That call has never been received, but for some reason, my thoughts keep telling me it will come.

04:00 hours arrives. No call. Nothing. I sigh with the relief that all will be well. My eyes can close once more. It's a chore to roll over and spoon without disturbing her. She has been patient with the wakeful nights. At least she doesn't mention it.

My phone rings.

I roll over and see the time, 04:02 hours. The office is calling. My perfect day is disrupted as the number flashes on the cell phone where it sits in the cradle. Why today?

The phone quiets as I grab it from the cradle. My feet find slippers, and without hesitation, out to the bedroom they lead me. The cat thinks I'm up to feed her and she rumbles down the stairs towards the kitchen. The bathroom is where I'm heading though.

"Hello?"

"Hello, Doctor Fergus?"

It really is a strange question when you come to think about it. This person has called my cell phone. Only two people live in this house and everyone knows it. So why do they believe someone else other than me would answer?

"Yes. The question, though, is who are you?" My voice is hushed, trying not to wake my wife.

"We have a 42."

You won't get the reference. Most people don't. It means someone found a planet killer.

"Are you sure?" Yes, I actually ask the question. Stupid, absolutely stupid. Of course he's sure. Why would he call if he wasn't sure?

"Yes, doc, we're sure. They verified it using Hubble."

"I'll be right in." Off goes the cell phone. There is scratching at the door and howling.

The howl turns to shock and is abruptly cut off.

"I got her."

I swear under my breath. The damn cat woke up the wife, and now she's going to want to know what's happened.

"I'm going to take a shower." My hand turns on the water. It thunders into the tub. "Go back to bed, I'll be home early."

"Let's get you some food." Her voice trails off.

I can hear her go downstairs over the sound of the water.

Get Going

The smell of coffee floats up from downstairs. God bless her, she turned on the pot. Every once in a while I'm surprised.

Clothes first. My hand hits the lights and there is my suit laid out for me with a bundle of fur on top of it. Reminds me of why I married her.

"Okay, Mitus. Off."

The cat just licks her leg. My head shakes. I reach out and move the queen out of the way in order to get dressed. It is 04:15 and time is running out. There is still another twenty minutes of driving ahead of me.

Mitus watches as I dress. She's my cat, and always wants to be near me. The stairs are close and once down them, I'm greeted with my wife's smile and a cup of coffee.

"I want you home early," she says, one hand holding her house coat closed and the other one smoothing my hair. She tugs at my beard. "You're getting a little salt in your pepper there."

"I love you too." I pull her close and kiss. She play-struggles and kisses me back. Arms hug me hard. "Hey, don't worry. Nothing's going to happen. Probably some big brass coming to see where the seven billion went this year."

"Yeah, right."

She can always tell when I'm lying, but what else is there to say? Honey, there's a huge asteroid, or even a rogue planet coming at us. Sure, that would go over really well.

She pushes away and gives me a stern look.

"Okay. I'll be back early."

She nods and gives me a peck on the cheek, then heads upstairs. The cat follows her.

"Love you."

"Love you too," she says.

I head out the door.

Just a Little One

It is still raining when I get out of the car. Not heavy, just enough to make you want to pull your clothes in around you. A rain that makes you shiver even though it's a mid-summer morning.

"Hi, doc." The guard recognizes me, but as usual I can't remember his name.

"Hi." My voice comes out like a squeak. The badge I carry slides over the reader and my smiling face is projected in front of the guard. The holographic image is just one of those things I'm still not used to. And the capture they did is terrible.

"You're here early."

It's like he wants to know something but is afraid to ask. He knows our facility scans space for threats but what kind, he's not sure.

He opens his mouth and speaks again. "There's a whole lot'ta guys upstairs."

"Yeah, early. Just a routine inspection of the facility by some brass."

He smiles at that. Guess I'm not as good a liar as I thought. The guard nods me through.

"Mr. Brodden is near the lift. Could you remind him not to smoke in the building?" He pressed a button and magnetic locks disengage allowing me to enter the facility.

Sam is in the lobby, pacing. He looks tired. Circles paint a bluish brown under his eyes. He sees me, stops, and comes forward.

"You took your time."

I don't let him draw me into the argument. "What is it we have, Sam."

"A problem. Let's get up to Big Ben." He fishes in his pocket and comes up with a pack of cigarettes. A shaking hand fumbles one out and puts the cancer stick in his mouth. "Want one?"

"Thought you quit?"

His head shakes. "Who the fuck cares."

Sam lights up, blowing smoke out and coughing.

"Those things will kill you."

"Not fast enough." He hits the call button and we wait for the elevator. I hope that it takes a while. Sam in the elevator is bad enough. He has a restless leg. The cigarette is the other. It's been fifteen years since my last puff, and the smell usually makes me sick.

He sees me holding back and butts the thing out.

"Sorry, forgot."

The doors open and we enter. He hits seven and the doors close. I'm happy they killed the elevator music last month. It took a year, but all the emails finally sank in.

"Tell me a little about what was found." The silence is something I hate.

"I was told not to say anything."

"If this is a surprise party…" The last one they pulled was over a year ago.

"No." His answer is too short to be a lie.

"Then what?"

The elevator slows and stops. Doors open to the main room. At this time of the day it should be empty, but right now it's full. Twelve people are packed into it. My thoughts about this being a drill left me right then and there. Even the director the director is there talking with a man wearing enough medals on his uniform to build a small car. The scent of sweat fills the air along with a stale cigar.

"He's here," Sam calls out. The room quiets, and Carl, the director, looks over and motions for me to join him.

"About time you showed up," Carl says. "Looking for the dramatic entrance?"

The conference room doors open up. Julie stands there and looks over the group. Once her eyes land on me she comes forward. She looks worried.

"Hi, doc, everything's ready," she says, not a hint of the usual smile.

"What's going on, Julie?"

She hands over a binder. On the front are the words "Little One". My eyebrow rises. The code name is something I thought up.

Julie is standing there, nodding. I purse my lips and she turns, leading me into the conference room. Everyone follows.

Heat hits me as I enter the room. Big Ben must be working overtime. Air conditioners are throwing cold out, but processing power generates heat, and Big Ben has processing power to spare, or that's what we were told two years ago when we started this project. Now, I look at the readouts and see he's running at high capacity. It's the upper limit, allowing for basic commands to be run when needed.

"Ben," I call out. "What's your status?"

"Hello, doctor." They programed a baritone voice into Ben, but his inflections are always off just a bit. "I'm operating at 87.23% capacity. CPUs 1-98 are calculating at 7.3 terahertz and the first seven banks of ram are dumping to disc. I'm 92% completed with the current calculations.

Estimated time to completion is twelve minutes and thirty seven seconds."

Julie guides me towards a seat near the head of the conference table and makes me sit down. There's another binder on the table labeled "Out There". My mind reels. The title sparks something in the back of my skull, and it is itching there.

I go to open the binder and spy Carl shaking his head; he points to the binder Julie had given me. Thumbing through the binder makes my head pound.

There is a plotted course. A projected path through the solar system is laid out. Size is estimated with a surface area of 17 million square kilometers. Mass at over 1.67 x 10^22 kg. Basically, it's the size of Eris. How did we miss it?

"Gentlemen," Carl says. "As you know we have a 42 alert. A planet killer."

Everyone starts talking at once. I scan through the binder for anything important. The heat is getting to me.

"Doc, you okay?" Carl asks.

I look up and see him staring at me. Concern is in his eyes.

"Yes, sorry. Just getting up to speed." My feet are under me quickly. "We have a planet killer coming at us. Preliminary information tells us it has the mass and size of Eris, our tenth planet, if you include dwarf planets. I always have. A planet is a planet. The trajectory shows we have three months at the object's current speed." I stop, and pinch the bridge of my nose.

"Ben, how far are you on those calculations?"

"Calculations are now finished, doctor."

Something tells me not to call them up. If it's not confirmed there is a chance it will not happen. There could be an error in the initial course projection, or maybe it's just a blob on the telescope.

No, I need to know for sure, and so does everyone else.

"Ben, display the data through the holographic unit in conference room one."

The table top glows briefly. Images in the form of the sun and planets are displayed. Each planet has its orbit shown. The main asteroid belt between Mars and Jupiter is also displayed along with the Trojan Asteroids, from the smallest rock to the largest boulder, tumbling in virtual space. Even the Kuiper belt encircles our solar system.

Just outside the Kuiper is a flashing dot. The date displayed is today's.

"I will move the time index forward." The days tick forward and the planets move about the sun. Little One moves forward through the Kuiper belt, striking several of the asteroids, spewing them into space. Thirty days and the rogue planet passes the orbit of Uranus, but the gas giant is on the other side of the sun. Thirty more days and the planet enters the asteroid belt, pushing its way from one side to the other, and making a tunnel through the orbiting debris field.

The asteroids from the Kuiper belt are striking planets and moons, throwing the small objects out of their own orbits. The planet wreaks havoc through the system. I shudder.

Three months, four days, nine hours and twenty-seven minutes later the rogue hits our moon. The display has increased in size to show the effects of the collision.

The moon pushes forward, the Little One having struck our only satellite square on. The collision slows the Little One slightly, delaying the strike, but the moon glances off Earth, taking a chunk out of the North Pole.

When the planet finally strikes Earth twelve minutes later, there is a cracking of the surface. Ben's voice interjects, "I have extrapolated the course of every object. The strike will happen within the shown timeline. Each spatial object is tracked from the start to finish. The destruction of Earth is predicted based on current knowledge of the planet's structure. I'm sorry, doctor." The planets dissolve and the calculations display before us. Reams of information flows as the computer dumps memory to make room for the next function we will ask it to perform.

Out There

Seven people sit with their mouths open. One runs to the door, probably trying to get to the bathroom, but fails. He vomits just as he exits the room. I watch a tear drop from Julie's eye.

"Doc," Carl said. "How accurate is this model?"

I know what he's doing. He wants a way out. Some type of possibility that the world will survive this disaster. It's unfortunate something like this could not be disregarded.

"Sorry, Carl, there's no mistake. Ben's got the biggest processing power available." I see my fingers playing with the binder labeled "Out There", and wonder what it is all about. "Remember Halley's comet? Ben's the one that predicted its destruction while everyone else predicted its return."

"I remember that, a few years before I came on board."

My eyes won't leave the binder now.

"Go ahead."

I look up and Carl's smiling. He's inclining his head towards the binder. I pull it towards me and start skimming it. My eyes widen in disbelief.

"When did this—" I start.

"It was my last directorship." Carl is grinning now.

"But when? How? Why haven't I heard of anything like this before?" My head is reeling now.

"I started project 'Out There' ten years ago," he says. "Each member of the United Nations has been syphoning money towards the project. Took us three years to get the plans drawn. Another four to build the facility. It surprised me how fast the parts came in. Some ordered through NASA, others from different country's space exploration arms. It was quite easy, really." His smile cuts through the cloud of people talking.

"Look," I say, standing. My body is craving fresh air. "I have no idea what this project's about. Really, the scale of this is phenomenal!" I'm waving the binder in front of me subconsciously. "How all of this was built without anyone knowing is just..."

"You skimmed it," he says to me. "There's no worry about it. Use the information and just follow the timeline on the last page."

The chime rings and Big Ben calls everyone back to the conference room. My hand turns the chair towards me, the tall, black back invites me to sit and be comfortable, but the feeling running up and down my spine is nothing like that.

"The floor is yours, Doctor." Ben turns off his speaker and I stand once again.

"It seems we have a way to survive, but not much time to do it in." I then start to lay out the plan in the binder.

Getting Ready

I can't believe how easily Julie transitioned from our small office to the big one in this new facility. The lack of windows unnerves me, personally. How people could work with the walls looming over them baffles my understanding.

Several other astrophysicists help me deal with all the details concerning the plan. This is beyond me. How did they think I could handle all the details involved? So much to do and so little time to do it in. Why couldn't we have found the 42 sooner? It really wouldn't have made any difference. We would have just pushed with less ferocity than we are now.

The piles of requisitions scream at me for attention. One finds its way in to my hands, and I read it with disinterest. Toilet paper, really? There has to be something else to ask for. Three tons, that's how much they're asking for. They must be elephants or something. What the hell would they be using that much for?

"Julie," I call out, hoping to pass on the need to investigate.

"Yes, doc?" she says when her face pokes into the room.

"Here." I hold out the requisition form to her. "Find out how many times section seven flushes the toilet and see if they really need so much ass-wipe."

She grabs the paper from me and chuckles. "I'll look in on it." I can see the question in her eyes.

"What?"

"Are you okay?"

"We've worked together for about twelve years now, right?" My fingers run thought my hair, scratching at an imaginary itch at the back of my skull.

"A little over, I'd say." Her eyes are full of concern.

"Have you even known me to be an administrator?"

She starts to giggle.

"Sorry, doc. It's just that for the last few days you've shuffled more paper and administrated this facility better than anyone. There's no one I could point to who would have done a better job." She flourishes the requisition form in front of her. "Most would have just signed off on this without even thinking."

My mind pictures Carl behind the desk with crates of toilet paper stacked behind him and I start to laugh.

"Carl, right?" Julie says.

"Yes. It's stacked—"

"—Behind him."

The headache starts to disappear. The levity is enough to break the ice. Standing, I make my way around the desk and take the requisition from her. "I'll take care of this."

She giggles her way back to her desk.

The hallway is inviting as a cave is to someone who's claustrophobic. I keep getting the sense that the world is about to collapse, and it's not that far off. We're all surprised that no one has found out our little secrete, that of the 42.

Maybe that's what they needed the toilet paper for. Build a little bouncing point for the impact zone.

One door keeps me away from the head of software development. Someone had a sense of humor, taping 'Super Geeks' over the actual department name with a drawing of a classic geek with a cap blowing in the wind. The pocket protector is a cute touch.

I reach out and open the door. Seven people are grouped around the large window decorating the wall. It's unbelievable that they have windows in their area and there's none in my office. Things will have to change.

There's a name on the requisition form. A Marcus Kollof.

"Who's Marcus Kollof, and why does he need so much toilet paper?" My voice has the desired effect.

The group breaks up and each head for their chairs, all except one. The red haired gorilla just turns and scowls at me. A thick Russian accent breaks through his lips. "Who says I'm full of der'mo?"

I step into the room and walk towards the window. "The one who approves your seat on her." One finger of my left hand points to The Hope down below.

Very few people have ever seen The Hope. The ship is huge. Enough to hold five hundred people and all the supplies needed to make their trip to Gliese.

We have five such ships ready to reach out to the stars. Each with the same experimental drive system they claim will allow us to surpass the speed of light. The bulk of each ship's drive system is already in space, hidden in a polar orbit behind large shields. If people look for them they will just see a black field.

The blunt nose of each ship arches back to the sleek body, and two large pods reach out from both sides. They collect hydrogen and transfer it to the engine for burning. The lines are bold enough to get lost in, but each ship has a Big Ben installed in its head. Nothing will stop us from surviving. Nothing, that is, except sloppy programming.

"Or better yet," I say. "The paper here says you are."

Marcus steps forward and snatches the requisition form from my hand. "Explain."

"You've requested 3 tons of toilet paper—"

"No, delo." His finger jabs the paper, almost puncturing it.

"Tons. That's what is says here."

"Delo. See, you have to see the py."

"Look, you've spelled it ton, and I can't approve that much. Redo it and put it in English. See the top here? All requisitions must be in English." I reach over and point out the instructions to him.

"Der'mo meshok!"

"What?" I say.

"Shit bag. Computer translates poorly." He smiles now, the gap between his front teeth showing. "Me full of shit."

"Just correct it." I start to leave but his meat hook of a hand lands on my shoulder.

"You need to see." He guides me to the terminal at his desk. "You Big Ben work good, but issues with calculation."

"What do you mean?" Something is telling me this is important, but there is only so much one can do.

"I link all Big Ben together. Good spectrum here not used. New information shows planet speeding up. Time not much." His smile is gone now, and the readout on the terminal is spewing out numbers.

"When one Big Ben made for American calculate, it make pretty picture for all to see. Not much time on real numbers, just lines in air to make happy." I'm leaning in now, seeing the figures come to the correct assumption. We have less time then we predicted.

We Meet Again

I'm tired.

After a long four hours of analyzing the data Marcus showed there was no dismissing the information. The planet was speeding up. It's our sun, and it took the combined processing power of the Big Bens to figure it out. No fancy graphics, just numbers. Numbers and the gravity well of our star.

Once everything was collated, a fast jet was prepared and my bags magically appeared in the passenger compartment along with a note from Julie. My wife will be waiting for me. It's been almost two weeks since I saw her last.

I board the plane and find the nearest seat to the front. My ass hits it and before the plane lifts off the tarmac my eyes close.

It's hard to know if someone else is on a plane with you when your eyes are closed. They don't open up again until two hours later, and not even then until an attendant shakes my shoulder. I must say, the tumble of her blonde hair is impressive, along with her striking blue eyes. All that and a military uniform as well. Enough rank symbols have been flashed in front of my eyes for me to know she's a captain.

"Doctor, we're about to land." She stops shaking me as my eyes open.

"Okay," I yawn. "Is there any coffee, Captain…"

"Jesper. Sorry, I don't drink coffee, and I don't think you'd like to drink what would pass for my coffee."

We hit turbulence and she moves quickly to the seat across the aisle. Her hands fumble with the belt before it snaps into place. With a tug, she tightens it.

"Fly much?" I ask. Her face is ashen.

"Last time I did we dumped into the Pacific." Her hands are straining on the armrest.

"How long ago?"

"Four years, eight months and twenty days ago."

"You keep count?"

"It's the last time I flew." She has an air sickness bag in her hand now.

I look around the plane. No one else is on board. "You're doing okay. We'll make it."

"That's what the pilot said. We'll make it. Next thing I know I'm shooting out of the cockpit with a rocket blasting me into the air. Do you know how cold the water is right after a spring melt? I do." Turbulence rock the plane.

The intercom comes to life. "We're landing in ten minutes. Fast approach protocol is approved. Please tighten your belts." The intercom snaps off.

"Fast approach?" I ask. Her eyes are closed now.

"Means we're aimed at the runway. He's going to burn off the altitude soon, take us right into the airport." She vomits into the bag.

The whine of the engines subsides and the plane's nose dips. A small TV on the bulkhead reads out the altitude and air speed. One is decreasing and the other is increasing. My stomach tries to climb out though my nose.

"In front of you."

I look over. She's holding another air sickness bag and pointing to the flap in front of her. "I'm not there yet."

We start leveling off, and a rumble shakes the plane as landing gear drops from the metal belly. My hands are now gripping the arm rests. The nose is up, the rear tires hit. It's the worst sound in the world, the sound of tires ripping across asphalt faster than they should be.

The sun is rising. Gold reflects off the tower's glass.

Once we're at the terminal, they rush us off the plane and through a blocked off section of security. It's the fastest I've been in and out of any airport. And before I know it, Captain Jesper has me by the elbow, moving us out to a waiting car. My bags are there. My wife is there. She rushes towards me.

She's in my arms before I know what's happening. The bear hug almost cracks my ribs. Her voice breaks the silence.

"I've missed you."

We lean in together. Lips meet.

Jesper clears her throat. "That's sweet."

I pull back and look into my wife's eyes. "I have a lot of meetings to go to, and the first one's in twenty minutes."

"Yes, I know. They told me. We get to catch up."

"Doctor, I've been assigned as your liaison with the brass," Captain Jesper says.

"Who are you?" My wife is looking over my shoulder.

"Captain Beatrice Jesper, you can call me Bes."

I'm surprised. "Beatrice?"

"You can call me Captain Jesper," she says, looking at me.

"Hi, Bes. I'm—"

"Sarah Fergus. Age thirty-seven. Doctorate in abnormal, cognitive and social psychology."

"You know a lot about me, it seems."

I turn towards the captain. "Well, if you must come with us…"

She nods and we all climb into the vehicle.

The driver gets us on the highway, then to the military base. Sarah has never liked fast moving vehicles. She tries to keep her eyes on me, but they wander to the road. I just try and hold onto her attention while lead foot moves us through traffic. Ten minutes later, we're pulling into the base, and it's guarded like Fort Knox.

Medals is waiting for us. He's wearing even more ribbons and dangling icons then the last time I saw him. Maybe a bus worth this time. Not one of them appears to be from combat.

The smile is plastic, his hand limp. My opinion of him is dropping by the moment. His badge hangs from the coat pocket. Billington, William. He's a General.

Jesper gets that ramrod look going as she salutes. Billington returns it with a limp hand. Sloppy. He reeks of stale cigar smoke and scotch. Must be nice.

Sarah takes the man's hand and I can see she's profiling him. Calculating eyes smile as her hand drops to remove his form her elbow.

"Welcome to Washington, doc."

"I have a lot of work to do. It would have been better to just come to the facility." Something tells me this man doesn't go anywhere for anyone.

"You live here, and so does your wife."

"We could have given her clearance to join me. Actually, that's a good idea. I want her to have clearance."

He smiles. "That's why she's here."

Sarah looks at me. "What's this all about?"

Billington puts his finger to his lips. "Not until you sign some papers."

I nod.

He leads us into the building, past more armed guards.

"They're a little paranoid here," Sarah says.

"You have no idea," I whisper back.

Into another office and we are directed to sit. Jesper just stands here, ramrod straight. A couple of MPs come in and take Sarah away. Billington tells me he'll make sure the interview goes well and to stay here. He leaves.

Jesper relaxes and looks at me. I shake my head.

"You do that a lot," she says.

"What?"

"Shake your head."

The statement bounces around in my skull. "I think it's better to shake my head then his." I cross my eyes. A little trick inherited from an aunt.

That gets me a smile.

"Do you report to him directly?"

She walks over to the chair next to mine. "No, thank God. I almost choke when his booze soaked breath hits me. He doesn't own a toothbrush from what I hear."

I chuckle.

"Did he earn all those medals or are they just for show?"

"Earned them, as far as being able to wear them. Most are from just being safe at the base when others went out to fight. All he had to do was be there for two weeks."

"And he gets a medal?"

"Ya, he gets a medal. Most soldiers don't wear theirs, but he does. All of them."

It's chitchat. We keep talking for a while, exchanging antidotes. I tell her how Sarah and I met, she tells me about her cats. Thirty minutes go by and Sarah comes back into the room, shaking.

She sits beside me and Jesper shoots up as booze breath comes into the room.

"She's legal," he says.

"You okay?" I take her hand.

A tear is in her eye.

"I-I can't believe it."

I reach for her hand.

"We have a few things to talk about." Billington sits behind the desk. "Jesper, relax."

"Yes, Sir."

"So, your supercomputer's not that super. Fudged the time frame by a month."

"With all due respect, General. Big Ben only had two hours of data to examine. Not much to tell the velocity of the 42, let alone know it was accelerating."

He nods. "Okay, doc. I'll give you that one. Are the ships ready?"

"No."

"Ships?" Sarah asks.

"There's a number of things not covered in the briefing, Mrs. Fergus."

"Project 'Out There' has five spaceships in the final stages of completion. We've been trying to finish everything off over the last few weeks." Sarah is staring at me. "Each will carry five hundred men and women to Gliese G. Everyone will be in suspended animation."

"And you've been involved in this for how long?"

"Only the two weeks." She squeezes my hand.

"How far?" she asks.

"20 light years. Gliese is in the constellation of Libra. Gliese G is in the zone."

Her eyes widen. "The Goldilocks Zone."

"We don't call it that. The habitable zone. Anyway, there are three planets that could sustain us, and it all depends on what we find when we get there. If we get there."

"What will stop us?" Sarah asks.

"Experimental drive systems, radiation, suspended animation, the unknown. Lots of issues. Hell, this is all a crap shoot anyway."

"But we'll survive." She is full of hope, anyone can see it. I'm no longer smiling, neither is Billington. Sarah is looking between the two of us. "We'll survive. Right?"

"The strongest have been picked for the trip," Billington says. "Couples in the right age and demeanor. All of them strong and capable of surviving off the land."

Sarah turns to me. "We'll survive. Right?"

A lump forms in my throat. I force a swallow and look down at the ground. "The human race will survive." My eyes meet Sarah's. "But we're too old to be picked for the flight."

Job Well Done

Two months have spun past so fast. We finally got the last of the ships ready. All the couples are now safe in suspended animation pods. Our five ships, all powered up and ready to go, sit upon the rail system. We'll get them up to Mach five before the chemical rockets ignite.

We're cutting it close. Only one week left. The 42 is visible in the sky now, both day and night. It was visible about two weeks ago, and the night Sarah saw it, she took her own life. No note. Nothing. She was living at the facility when it happened. I came home to our billet and her feet swung a foot off the ground. Tears streaked my face for a long time. Julie found me the next day, holding Sarah and rocking back and forth.

She helped me. Cleaned me up. Got Sarah ready for the MPs. We buried her at the base of the rail system. Jesper was there, along with Carl and Billington. The service took thirty minutes and we returned to work.

The countdown hits three and the power going through the rail shakes the whole countryside. Black smoke is pouring out of the fifty generators built on the site. Just enough power is generated to get the ships moving and keep the lights on.

My stomach flips as the five ships start moving down the ten kilometers of rail. At the end, the chemical rockets ignite and the ships arch to the heavens. Cheering rises from the control room.

We watch as the ships make their way out of the atmosphere, connect with the main drive systems in orbit and flush the first ton of hydrogen to accelerate. I say a silent prayer.

Two months. That's all it took us. Over a thousand technicians, welders, electricians and programmers have made it possible.

Hubble tracks the ships as they speed away. Their image becomes fuzzy as their speed passes the fastest man has ever gone before. Then nothing. No light is traveling fast enough to bounce off them. They have hit light speed.

Humanity has reached the stars. Hopefully, we will survive.

The Cross

"Go ahead, take it." Dillon holds out the cross to me. The gold gleams in the candlelight. The cross is smaller than I would think, only a few inches in length, but heavy with the faith it represents. Dillon's smile arches across his broad face, a glint of sweat trailing down the side of his head.

"Are you sure?" My hand reaches out with more hesitation than I intend.

"Yes, you deserve it." Again, Dillon bobs the cross up and down. It is like a carrot, pulling my faith forward toward the light that shines inside it. "You can always give it back."

It's not a decision one makes easily. To take your faith in hand and return it if it does not suit you. Take the cross and hang it around your neck. Read the faith to the faithful and forgive them of their sins. Really, it is easy to do.

"I have your robe ready as well." His eyes flicker to the chair. A small bundle of brown cloth lays there. The green of his eyes center on me again, as if he sees inside my very soul.

My hand shakes as I touch the metal. It is warm, probably from his grip, but nevertheless it is warmer than my hand. With a deep breath, I wait. Sparks dance at the edge of my vision. The feeling that my faith is on the line drains the last resolution within me. A decision must be made, and his eyes tell this loud and clear.

"I guess—"

"Don't guess," Dillon says. His eyes are tender, almost loving. The voice is strong, no longer soft. He wants me to make up my mind. Come forward and take the charge. It is a hard life he wants me to take on. Wake, pray, clean, pray, farm, pray, sleep, repeat. He wants me to live in a small village, to have supplicants of maybe twenty souls, no more. Read to them, for most cannot. There would be nothing for me to own, no land, just something the church would lend me in order for the daily bread to be grown. Grinding the grain was the church's responsibility, but that meant the one leading the followers would do it. That would fall on my shoulders again.

"Yes. No guessing. I understand." My thumb closes on the top, fingers curling underneath it. "And what else do I need to know?"

"There will be a tithe that you will collect. Monitor what each gives, and ensure they are not holding back. I admit your life will not be easy. At first you may want to leave the order and take what you have collected. But your immortal soul would be scarred forever. Passage into the afterlife could not be allowed. Purgatory would be your punishment. If you have second thoughts, I suggest you return to the sanctum sanatorium and pray for guidance."

Yes, I have second thoughts, but not about faith. Father sent me to the church. It was his way of getting rid of a child who wanted to know too much. There was no school to teach me how to read. And at the age of seven, father knew I would amount to no good staying with him. Even my sisters, all twelve of them, had left the family farm before they were sixteen. Father wanted one more child, but when I came out, so did part of my mother's insides as well.

Father was convinced it was my inherent curiosity which led her to die. He said I pulled her insides out because of what was in me. A demon, maybe. But he was not an educated man, and didn't have the intelligence to understand that at forty-one, mother was just too old to have another child.

Dillon lets go of the cross.

It does not fall to the ground. My fingers flex. Yes, it feels good. And, with this simple act, I commit myself to the order. Dillon smiles.

"See, not so hard." His other hand is on my shoulder. He squeezes. "There is much you need to know. But first there are some vows."

"Put on the robe and join us at the top of the spire. Don't shave or clean, just put on the robe and climb the stairs." He leaves.

The chill of the air makes me shiver. I look at the bed, the one thing that never changed in my life. Straw on some boards; a wool blanket over top. Boiled goose feathers in a linen sack serve as a cushion for my head. Don't dawdle; there is no one to chew the fat with here. Not that we had any pig belly. No one did.

My fingers move to the ties holding the smock at my shoulders. The light fabric falls to the ground.

There is a small loop at the top of the cross, and the robe on the chair has some twine on top of it. It is coarse in my hands, but I manage to thread it through the loop. The two ends meet in front of me, and the thought of tying a knot by joining them reminds me of a devil's knot. The twine comes out of the loop easily. The thoughts of placing the cold cross on my chest are something that tells me to change the way it is done. With the twine on the table, the idea comes to me. It is now doubled, the two ends running together. The knot sits perfectly there, without causing concerns.

The double end goes through the loop, and then it doubles under. The cross is now held with a perfect circle, but not within it. The faith is unbroken.

I do not know how much time passes. The cross lies on the table in front of me. It's perfect, glinting in the small light.

My mind made up, the robe falls over my head, fitting loosely on shoulders not willing to accept the role thrust upon them.

There's a rope on the chair. It was under the robe. It's to place around the waist, gathering the sides together in order for it to stay snug. The rope goes around me, tight but comfortable.

Nothing is stopping me now. Everything is in place. Dressed, perfect, ready. The cross sparkles. It wants to be around my neck, but there is hesitation again. Maybe it's just the want to shave. The prickly feeling of growing hair is bothering me to such a degree that scratching comes to mind. No, it's something that cannot happen. No shaving, no itching, just acquiescence.

I move from the spot, heading towards the door. Left hand scooping up the twine, the cross following, dangling inches off the ground. Open the door, move down the corridor, through the great hall. Many squires look up, wanting to know where the lonely acolyte is going.

No looking back. Stay the course. The cross swings back and forth. The weight of it pulls my arm. Faith should not be this hard. It should be easy, something to cherish, to hold in your arms. Why do we make walking in the shadow of our God difficult?

There are the stairs, just steps in front of me. Nothing is left now but to climb them. Go to the top, and expose myself to the wind. Feel the hand of God touch my soul and cleanse the last remnants of evil from me. My eyes search down to the small gold emblem of faith hanging on the string. It has to go around my neck, there is no more waiting. I cannot show up without it there, the others will be disappointed; they will not let me continue on the journey.

The twine pulls down on my neck. Hundreds of pounds suspending from the small cord make my movements difficult. Yes, I do want to scream, to trumpet my inner desire to be free of it to the world. This is the one thing that takes me beyond understanding, to a place where others will look up to me with respect and admiration. Why must this happen now? Not worthy. It is going through my mind. Who really is a worthy one? When someone says there is faith beyond question we question them. Are they insane? The true believers always are a little on the bent side. Not the sharpest pins in the hat. But why me?

There are fifty stairs behind me before my mind wakes up from the endless questioning. Blind faith leads me up the stairs. Only two hundred left to go. Will I make it?

Will I stumble, end the metronome of life that strikes back and forth? No, my luck would not be so great. We all take what life gives us and try to make the best of it. They tried to teach us to live life to the fullest, but when there is no time to live life to the fullest, what can you look forward too? Soil under your fingernails? A hungry stomach before bed? No one to share your life with but the God you have chosen to honor? There has to be something more.

Only fifty more steps to go. A small light above casts shadows against the wall. The echo of my footsteps against the cold stone mocks me, crying out to end the folly. Return to your room, it says. Be warm, it says. Sell the cross, it says. Little does it know that no blacksmith would melt a cross of the faith. Not one like this, anyways. Fire would hardly soften it. A hammer will dent before this symbol of faith is marred.

The cross swings forward and back, slamming its heavy burden on my chest. Faith has no weight, they say. But how many of them truly say that? Hundreds? Thousands? Weight would be nothing if it was shared by so many.

I am at the top now. A small ladder made from tree limbs reaches to a hole in the ceiling. One hand over another and I reach the top. Strong hands take hold of my arms and lift me unto the vastness of the night sky.

A slight wind passes with just enough strength to flutter the robes of all present. I count twenty. All of them are old, their beards hanging down from their chins, waving in an uncontrollable dance. They each have hoods drawn up to cover their faces in shadows. Hands in the sleeves before them, they seem to be staring into me, stripping away the robe and skin to see the very essence of my being. All save one.

The stranger. The one I have never seen before. His face is clean, and eyes crystal clear with a blue so pure it looks like ice. Short hair on his head hardly moves in the wind. His cowl is down, not putting him in shadows. Arms, strong and friendly, draped at his side. His hands seem gentle, almost caring. The one corner of his mouth raised in a smile. "Are you ready?"

I have never heard such a voice. Clean, clear, simple. The gentle way it moves through the air puts me at ease. Nothing could go wrong with a voice like that to guide you. A slight nod of response is all I can do.

"Good. You will kneel before your God." He turns and spreads his hands towards the heavens. Twelve old men kneel in supplication, their hands moving forward before them.

Before my legs finish bending, I hear his voice once again in my ears. "You will not kneel."

My legs stop, and slowly straighten. A shiver runs up from the bottoms of my feet to the top of my head. He wants me to face God on my own terms. But who am I to do this? I am nothing. A lonely little existence that is pushing towards the top of the spire. With a heart heavy with worry, I look around to those before me. They are all kneeling still, their foreheads to the stone.

"You will disrobe now." It is a command. Before my mind can react, I find the knot of the rope and untie, the clothing I wear drops to my ankles. He turns to me once again.

Have you ever been part of a visual examination where someone studies every single inch of your body with their eyes? The feeling of being naked in front of him is overwhelming. It is beyond what I can explain. He bores into me, through me, making me feel beyond naked. The cross, the only protection against the elements, hangs low, covering my sternum.

"Yes, you will do quite nicely." Both corners of his mouth are smiling now. "How old are you, child?"

"Si-si-sixt-teen," my voice offers. The cold of the wind is biting through me now.

"A fine age to be enlightened. How long have you been at the monastery?"

"Nine years, sir." My teeth chatter. Goose bumps adorn my skin from the cold.

His smile fades. Anger flashes in his face. The blazing sun erupts from his eyes as he walks forward to stand in front of me. The rankness of his breath makes me think of horrors in my dreams. The thought that this man, who looked kind and good, would be filled with such foulness to reek of death and decay bothered me to no end. My recoil must have been obvious, for his hands are now on my shoulders, shaking.

"What is wrong with you? Have you no love for your God? I am here. Flesh reborn in this body. You will love me!"

The spittle cast from his mouth stings my skin. It is poison. My desire is to recoil, but his eyes, those fiery red eyes hold me. The blue of ice is gone from them, and I wonder where.

"You are promised to me. Now, you will submit."

His hand touches my belly, his hands heading down. No one has touched me there. No one. I realize what father said to me years ago; to not let anyone touch me below until the marriage was complete. Keep chaste. Surely he did not mean my God? But what God would need to do this to me? Surely this was not meant to be.

"Never!" My scream echoes through the night and my knee strikes the soft flesh between the legs of the man in front of me. One monk looks up at the sound of my defiance and grimaces. He then realizes the pain in the man's eyes and stands.

"A God would not feel pain," he says, trembling.

Others look up, seeing God grabbing himself and doubling over. Vomit on the stones in front of him tells a tale. I look down and the cross is glowing.

"A God would have known about the actions of a pure heart." The chants rise up from the mouths of them all. They converge on us, and rough, old, wizen hands lift the God into the air and toss him over the side. His scream fills the air.

When he hits the ground, I do not know. His scream seems to go on forever. One of the priests places my robe about my shoulders, patting my back lightly.

The cross is no longer heavy. It feels light as a feather. I look to the priest. "My vows?"

He chuckles. "We have no vows here. We keep the faith; that is all."

"But I was told—"

"To be ready, and you were, my dear." The old man takes my hand. "The faith believes in all of us. I guess that is why the madness took him." He inclines his head in the direction of the edge of the tower. I look over to the ground below. "He believed so much that his belief swallowed him. Now he is no longer. I am surprised that one so young as you saw it first."

"No, not really. A God would have no need to see me naked. No need to touch me." My hand clasps the cross between my breasts, my blonde hair whipping about in the increasing wind. "He would already be inside of me if... My faith is inside of me, so God is there as well."

He smiles as his head tilts slightly. "You are strong of faith, my child. A woman to lead all the women of our order."

Equinox

Tanis studied the charts spread on the table. His eyes watered from strain and he pinched the bridge of his nose.

"The stars are lining up tonight," he said to the acolyte, who bowed. "Are the stones cleaned?"

"Yes your eminence, with sand from the foot of the mountains, as you instructed."

"And the water?"

"From the drippings of the receding ice, your eminence."

Tanis stood, his knees creaking. The wool of his shift still kept him warm from the bitter cold wind sneaking through the castle. Ten paces away, a fire roared, fighting the chill of the night for dominance. He walked to the fire, speeding his fingers to feel the heat from the blaze. *I am old. This may be the last ceremony I can perform.*

"Your eminence?" the acolyte asked.

"Yes, Stal?"

"The woman, are we supposed--"

"Are you questioning the scriptures?"

"No your eminence."

"Then keep your tongue still." He moved from the fire to the window, rubbing his hands together, hoping the circulation would warm his fingers. "Besides, the night brings us the sign. The star burns bright in the sky."

"Yes, your eminence."

The old man scratched his face through the whiskers on his face. He dreamed of a perfect time, the balance of night and day. "We must meet this sacred time with the appropriate sacrifice. The newborn will come forth, and the prophecy fulfilled."

"Your eminence?"

"Yes Stal." The old man stared out the window at the clear night sky, his breath frosting on the glass.

"Do we really have to? I mean, the girl is only--"

"Pregnant? How else could she bring forth new life?" He turned to face the young man. *He is so young, will he really understand?* "We have very little time left. Help me, Stal. My legs are weak, and the stairs are so difficult for me."

He held out his arm, and Stal took it, supporting the weight of the old man with ease. *I have lost much weight this winter. Will I survive another winter?*

They left the warmth of the room and down the stairs. The walk was slow, and pain shot from his knees down to his toes and up to his hips with every step down he took. The old man was pleased with Stal, who took his time in helping. They reached the landing area and he paused, taking a deep breath and leaning more on the acolyte. Once his knees stopped screaming, he motioned to Stal to help him move down the last of the stairs.

Tanis saw the faces of other acolytes watch them approach the main floor, and wondered what they saw. Did their eyes see a gentle soul who guided their order from spring to spring, or did they see an old man, no longer able to support himself, a life ending as winter is ended by spring? He signed with the knowledge he would never know.

"She is on the altar, holding as best she can, your eminence," said Jarvis, another acolyte, who took care of the woman and made sure she was comfortable.

"My dagger, has it been sharpened?" He held out his hand expectantly.

"Yes, your eminence." The dagger was presented hilt first to the man, and he pulled it from the sheath. His fingers tested the edge, shaving skin off the tips.

"This is fine," he said, putting the weapon in his belt. "Take me to her."

The acolytes gathered in a row, lifting cowls over their heads, hiding their faces. The men moved as one through the castle gates, towards the sacrificial altar high on a hill.

Will he make it on time? Tanis looked at the sky as he walked, seeing the brightening of the eastern horizon. And as he turned his head, he saw the star, marking the day as it did every year. *We must hurry,* and he quickened his steps.

The obelisks stood tall, black as the coal from the heart of the mountain. The blocks of stone stood exactly seven feet tall, and two feet square. They encircled a flat marble slab, angled to catch the first rays of the sun on the day of equality, when day and night were the same. Upon the alter laid a woman, who's skin was the color or ebony. She was naked, a belly heavy with child. She gritted her teeth in pain, as two acolytes held her legs together. She panted, the throws of childbirth upon her.

"The time is upon us," Tanis proclaimed. The acolytes started to chant, and the woman's legs released. "A sign, the sun rises in the east."

The woman screamed, her body contracting. Tanis heard the acolyte who stood at her head, soothe her, whispering, "You may push now. The child must be out of you quickly."

Tanis raised his arms and turned to the rising sun.

"Stal, come stand beside me, my son." A pain raced across his left side, a dagger of his mortality.

"I am here, your eminence."

"Do not let me fail."

"I won't, your eminence."

Tanis turned to the woman, her legs spread and body birthing a child. Shadows receded. He drew out the dagger. An acolyte stood at each side of the woman, ready to receive the child. Tanis turned his head and saw the top of the sun crest the horizon, as pain raced down his left arm. *No! I will survive.*

"Your eminence," Stal said, looking at his master. "Are you--"

"Help me, Stal…One life…One soul…the child…it must be born free," he gasped, as he pushed the dagger into Stal's hand.

"But , your eminence. You are--"

"Attend the child, fool. It must be free!" He fell to his knees, his head turned up to Stal, pleading.

"I…yes, your eminence."

Tanis smiled. "You will…replace me…you a…are your eminence now. Free…the…child!"

The acolyte stepped back, and Tanis watched as he strode to the woman, pulled the baby from her and used the blade to cut the cord of life. He nodded, knowing the flame was passed. And Stal took the infant in his hands and turned. Tanis fell to his side, heart bursting from his chest, as Stal raised the child to the sun as it crested over the horizon.

"The old is dying, and winter is leaving. The Equinox of life is once again upon us as the master passes the flame to his student." Stal lowered the child into an embrace, his eyes fading with age. He could feel his beard grow, and magic spread out. His life move forward as a flood of memories passed to him from his master. The circle of life passed to him from his eminence, and the babe grew heavy in his arms. The child was ten now, as the sun started to climb the sky. He felt his legs weaken, and back bend. His knees groaned with the strain of supporting his body.

A hand reached out, taking his arm, strong, solid and unyielding. Stal looked over and his mind whirled. *I am no longer Stal*, and he reached up to feel the itch of his beard. He looked over at the child who was no longer a child, a grown man now. *My name is Tanis, and he is Stal.*

"Take me to my room, Stal," Tanis said.

"Yes, your eminence," Stal said, taking the arm of his master.

Ark One

They made the walls white, just like the ceiling and floor. It is meant to show the purity of our mission.

Jennifer is in the chair beside me, an exact duplicate of mine. They cradle our bodies, enveloping and protecting us against the acceleration of the ship.

Thirty decks of cryogenically frozen humans rely on us to be perfect. Three thousand souls need us to be perfect. The human race is hoping we succeed.

The panel in front of me scrolls lines of information on its black surface, telling me everything is running within operational parameters. The ship, the slender mass of white metal they christened Ark One, is traveling near the speed of light. We are pushing the envelope of science to the breaking point. Ark One has been accelerating for two weeks now. Relatively speaking, it has been over 100 years on Earth.

I reach out my hand, searching for a touch from Jennifer. She is just within reach. Our fingers intertwine and her hand is welcoming. Warm. Tender.

We were made for this job. We are spliced. We are genetically engineered. We are perfect.

The stigma against our creation started before we were born. Norms marched on the research buildings holding signs, quoting Scripture, claiming we would take food off their tables. Programs explained we were made only for the task we do now, to stay awake while they are sleeping.

Twenty years ago, relative to our time, blanks were captured. Unfertilized eggs. DNA was pulled from them in laboratories and anomalies were sectioned out. Perfection was introduced. Eyesight, memory, coordination, strength, intelligence. Everything increased to the limits of flesh and bone.

I let go of Jennifer's hand and tap a few commands out on my panel.

"You going for a walk?" she asks.

"A run." I lean over and kiss her forehead. "Back in less than a year."

She laughs. "Well, you'll have to go at least two decks down..."

"Relatively?" I ask.

"It'll be about a year." She turns her attention back to the panel in front of her.

I swing open the rear hatch and enter the corridor that stretches down the length of the ship. Handholds greet me. They are recessed into the walls, spaced evenly from the Bridge to Engineering. On the forth deck my run begins.

There's not much to see. White walls with tanks of frozen people line the corridor. Small readouts projected in the air above the torso tell me who they are, what they do, how old, gender, married or single. Just about everything but how they feel about being in the care of a splice. The tanks have a small cut away widow where you can look at the face of the person. We have stared at each one of them, wondering what makes us so different.

The ship is not large. It takes five laps to make a kilometre, so I count each time I pass Smith's pod. Music starts to float in the air. Jennifer must have piped it in. Some artist from the mid-21st Century. No singing, just music.

Twelve laps and something's wrong. I notice Parker's pod is cracked open. I stop.

The readout shows his heart rate is increasing. The pod is in recovery, letting fresh air in and cycling the drugs from his system. I reach out and tap the comm unit on the pod. "Need you down here."

"What's wrong?" Her response is clipped. I must have interrupted her.

"Parker's awake."

Her pause is a deafening silence. "He's awake?"

"His pod's open and the system is cycling out the drugs." I reach forward and tap the wall panel to start a diagnostic. "The readout says there's an issue in the main processor for his unit. We'll have to replace it."

"I'm coming down."

Our lives are full of pauses. It takes her just over a minute to make it to the deck. I keep monitoring Parker's pod, waiting for something to go wrong. Nothing does.

"He awake yet?" Jennifer asks as she comes down the corridor.

"Not yet. He's just about at the right temp." I tap out another command and numbers appear. They are counting down from 20.

"What are we going to do?"

I look around. There is a small pack of clothes strapped to the side of the pod. I open the pack and pull out the jumpsuit. "Here's some clothes for him. We'll have to repair the unit. Can't do much until he's awake. Think he'll be hungry?"

She shakes her head. "Bet he throws his stomach."

Two steps back. No, take another one. "How far can they throw?"

"Oh, it won't be much. They were fasting for 24 hours before freezing." She smiles. "Relax. If he throws it'll only be water."

I smile, take her hand, and kiss it. This trip would have been horrible without her. Yes, two weeks is not a long time but we have a lot of time left. Time dilation sucks, but only for those whom you leave behind. Jennifer and I have no one on Earth. We're spliced. We're made for each other.

"I'll grab some food out of the galley."

"Oks. I'll monitor him." She turns to the pod and I make my way to the handholds. The galley is on the second deck, above our living quarters. The lights turn on as I enter, and the warm voice of Sally greets me.

"Good afternoon, Alex, are you hungry?" Sally turns on the catering unit and a menu displays in the air above it.

"No. One of the pods malfunctioned and we'll need to repair it. The occupant is waking up. It would be nice to have some water and food for him." I walk past the catering unit to the water dispenser.

"Ice chips and water." There is a sharp grinding noise and a small bag of chipped ice drops, followed by a bag of water.

"It is suggested to get the passenger back into the pod as soon as possible."

I grab the bags. "Is there any problem?"

"It is suggested to get the passenger back into the pod as soon as possible."

Should have figured it out. Sally's not the smartest AI on the ship. She's only the cooking computer, so very limited in vocabulary. I'll speak to Mother back on the Bridge to get the answer.

With water and ice in hand, I go back to the pod. Jennifer has the whole unit open, and Parker is sitting up with the jump suit on. She is wiping his brow and holding his hand. His hair is disheveled and a rough growth of whiskers speckle his chin. Heavy bags of dark skin pull at his eyes.

"He threw a little, but there was nothing in his stomach to come up." She smiles. "He needs something to drink."

"Sally said just ice at first." I hand over the bag of ice. "Watch his intake to make sure he doesn't drink too much too fast."

I turn, heading back to the bridge.

"Where you going?" Jennifer asks.

Do I tell her? We've never lied to each other before. "Just have to ask Mother a question." I hurry to the handholds and make my way back to the bridge.

The chair supports me as I lay there tapping in commands. After a few seconds, access to Mother is granted. Her smiling face appears on the view screen in front of our seats. The gray hair in a bun is set off by the large glasses they put on her image. Pencil-thin eyebrows top off the picture.

Her eyes twinkle as she focuses on me, but I know it's just programming.

"Yes, Alex?"

"Why do we need to get Parker back into cryo quickly?" Nice simple question.

"Because he's a born." Simple response but it makes no sense.

"I don't understand. Why?"

"Because he's a born. A natural. Not like you. His needs will overcome what can be given to him. Remember when you were awakened, Alex?" Her tone is nice and calm. "You were born the size you are now. You've never known the hardships of growing up, of becoming the man you are. This Parker grew up on Earth. Children on Earth are subject to problems. They are damaged psychologically no matter how you look at it."

Still not a straight answer, but something that will have to do. Mother has that look in her eye that tells me she will not extrapolate on the answer. "Oks. I'll get his pod up and running in a zip."

"I'll monitor the repairs. Do your best." And with that, her image dissolves.

I look at the time. Twenty minutes have passed. Another 30 days for those on Earth. Soon we will be so close to the speed of light that every minute on the ship will be a year for those we left behind.

Time to head back. I get up and move to the handholds, making my way down. When I hit the fourth deck Jennifer has Parker sitting up and drinking water. Something is different.

"He's not able to talk yet." Jennifer pulls away the water bag and she lifts an ice chip to his lips. "He threw a little after you left but has kept down a lot since."

"Can't talk?" I ask, looking at Parker.

He clears his throat and lets out a husky sound. It's an attempt to speak, but the tube that was down his throat probably scratched him.

"Don't talk." Jennifer is holding another ice chip out for him. He takes it. "And don't you make him talk," she says, glancing sideways towards me.

"Sure. Mother wants him back in the pod zip. We need to get him out of it so I can run a diag and find out what's going on." I walk toward the pod, hand unlatching the side. "Help me get this thing off him."

Jennifer and I remove the front of the pod, freeing Parker from his coffin. He smiles and starts to speak, but mostly air escapes his mouth.

"Don't speak. We'll be able to talk once you've healed." Jennifer feeds him another ice chip. "And once you can keep the water down, we'll get you a good meal."

Parker smiles and takes Jennifer's hand as she leads him out of the pod. His legs are shaky, and at one point he almost goes to his knees. I turn my attention back to the pod. There is an odour coming out of it. Some musk mixed with an acidic smell. Something strange happened here.

I tap out a few commands and find that board 23 in the base unit is the one malfunctioning. My hand finds it and with one tug it is free. The board is a little wet, and there are burn marks around three processors.

"Got the problem." I hold up the board.

"Do we have spares?" Jennifer asks.

"Down in Engineering." I'm out of the pod now, glad for the fresh air. "It's all damp down there."

"Could have been a leak." Jennifer turns to Parker. "You feeling better? Can you walk?"

He nods. She helps him stand. "I'll get some food in him. You head down and get the parts."

It's not alright, but what else can I say. "Oks. See you in a few."

The Engineering deck is dirty. Jennifer never comes down here. She thinks it's my world. I don't mind getting dirty, as long as a shower is nearby.

Right now I'm looking through the spare parts section, trying to find a replacement board. I've had no luck so far, and this is the third time looking through it.

I look up and see the grease-covered walls laughing at me. "Really? Is there not one replacement for this part?"

There is no answer. Nothing new. Even Mother doesn't come down here.

With no boards, I look at the CPUs. Maybe just replacing them will do the trick. A new hunt begins.

The first two come into my hands quickly, and the third is there, just within reach. Only two things left to do, confirm and repair. I stand up and walk to the work bench, the treasures still in my hands.

At the workbench, I punch up the codes. "Mother, I need you to test these CPUs."

There is a whirling sound as a reader protrudes from the wall. "Place the first one in the reader, Alex." Her voice is calm, but without her face floating in front of me I feel disjointed. "Have you verified the numbers?"

"Yes, two ZD55685 CPUs. Low profile. One ZR44355 Cross Fire. They look good." I place the first CPU into the reader.

"This CPU is good. Please replace it with the other ZD55685."

Without hesitation my hands swap out the units.

"This CPU is good. Please remove it and place the ZR44355 in the reader."

I swap the two.

"This CPU is damaged. One prong appears to be disconnected. Place the unit on the bench."

Frowning, I remove the CPU and place it on the bench. All 2,048 pins stare up at me. "I don't see anything wrong with this chip."

"Find the orientation mark. Two rows down. Five pins in."

"I see it. Looks like it's bent a little bit. Could have broken the molecular bonds. Think we can fix it?"

She's splitting her processor time. Sure, Mother's a super computer, more memory and power than the big server farms in the early 21st Century, but there are limits. Especially when you ask her to answer something concerning the unknown factor like I just did. Still, you would think she'd answer a little faster.

"You have the necessary skills to complete this repair, Alex. I believe you can fix the unit."

It only takes 20 minutes and the CPU passes the test. I remove the old CPUs from the board and insert the replacements. A quick flip of the levers and they are locked into place.

With the treasure in my hand, I make my way towards the galley. My stomach rumbles, reminding me it is dinner time. With luck, there will be something good to eat.

Laughter floats down to me as the galley approaches. Jennifer is happy about something from the sound of her voice. There is another laugh there; it must be Parker.

The rest of the rungs pass quickly and the galley is there. So are Jennifer and Parker. They are sitting at one of the tables, plates in front of them. It looks like she ate without me. This is the first time since we were awakened that she has eaten without me. Even during our training, we always ate together. We are a matched pair. Created for this journey. There is a strange feeling growing inside me.

"…And that is when he called the roll!" Parker says. He laughs. Jennifer laughs. I don't.

Jennifer sees me and waves. "Hi, Alex."

I nod, and make my way to the food dispenser.

"I owe you," Parker says. His voice is stronger now. It seems he just needed to get out of the pod to feel better. "My name's Frank. I'm the genetic engineer for the colony."

"I know, Mr. Parker." A latch clicks and my hand opens the drawer to remove dinner. There is not a lot on my plate.

"Call me Frank, please."

"We're not allowed to." I turn and he is right there, blocking my way to the table. "Excuse me, sir."

He frowns, eyes searching my face. Maybe he's upset with me. Good.

"I'm sorry?"

Jennifer stands and walks over to us. "He's right, Frank. They used behavior modification to keep us from calling the geneticists by their first names."

He turned to her. "But you do."

"Yes, but I didn't know what you did until just now. Alex was told before he got to know you."

My voice is louder than I expect. "But I don't know him."

"He is right here," she says. "You can get to know him now."

"I'm willing," Frank says.

"I have work to do." I move around him and to the table. Food helps me think, and I need to think with the board in my hands, examining the repair.

Jennifer comes over and hugs me. "I'll see you on the Bridge." She turns to Parker. "Let me show you the Bridge."

It's the smell of urine that wrinkles my nose. Parker's pod is disgusting compared to the rest of our ship. Ark One is clean, sterile, and white. Parker is dirty, full of germs, and has a dark skin colour. He does not clean up after himself, and Jennifer is starting to pick up his habits. I realized it when their plates were left in the galley for me to clear.

The board slides into its slot with a click. I get up.

"Mother, run diagnostics on this pod."

"Diagnostics failed. Run up sequence halted on command 7763."

"Display overhead." Where the medical display was, a new readout shows. Intricate overlays of circuits and diagrams. Command 7763 flashs. "Which board is that?"

"Board eight, section four processors two through seven."

My hand reaches inside the guts of the pod. One, two, three, four, five, six, seven… No eight. "It should be here. Mother, display location of board eight."

The overhead changes to show the location of board eight. My hand is hovering exactly where it should be. Nine is there, along with ten and 11, but no eight. I pull out my arm and stick my head into the access hole. Eight is missing.

"Mother, do we have a replacement board eight for the cryogenic pods?"

"Board eight of the standard startup diagnostic unit is a one-time system startup diagnostic board. No replacements are in inventory."

My head is shaking. "Why?"

"Deemed not necessary because it would only be used during startup of a cryogenics pod."

"Can we fabricate one?"

"The necessary parts are not in inventory."

"Can we use one from another pod?" It's the last chance.

"The boards are interchangeable between pods."

Triumph. He can be put back to sleep soon. "How can I access the board of a pod currently in use?"

The display swirls into a manual showing the access point. The only access point. It is through the interior of a pod.

"Mother, do we have a spare pod on board?"

"All pods are currently in use. One pod under repair."

This pod. I have to revive another person in order to put Parker back to sleep, and that other person would be awake. Something that does not appeal to me. "Mother, can we not rig something up to take its place?"

Long pauses are not something that Mother does. She's a very powerful computer, and she runs the whole ship without any issues. So when she does not answer right away, I grow worried.

The com unit sounds; it's Jennifer. "Alex, are you running a diagnostic on Mother?"

"No, she's extrapolating on a problem."

"Frank here. Anything I can help with?"

It surprises me. Why does he have to tell me who he is? Does he think there is someone else on the ship besides the three of us? "No, Mr. Parker. There is no genetic engineering needed down here."

There is a pause before Parker responds. "Understood."

The comm unit switches off.

I spend another three hours working on bypassing the system. Each time progress is made something else causes the unit to halt startup. It all comes down to board eight. We even fabricated the basic board, but the processors we needed were not in the stores. We cannot fabricate the processors.

The comm unit sounds. It is Jennifer. "Dinner time. Are you going to meet us in the galley?"

Us.

It is a strange sound. She asks if I could "meet us" in the galley. It used to be "meet me." So it came down to this. We are no longer the "us" she refers to. How can I really respond to this question? To be ousted from my companion by some normal.

"Are you there?"

"Yes. I'll be up there soon." I cut the com off and throw the pliers to the floor. "Mother, extrapolate the psychological effects of three crew members for the remaining journey."

There is a pause but not as long as the other one. "Crew rations are balanced for two."

"What does that mean?"

"Crew rations are balanced for two."

I don't know what she means by this statement. Food is not the question. My mind is wondering what effect having another person to interact with will have on the balance between Jennifer and me. I didn't ask about…

Food. The food is balanced so Jennifer and I will have enough food for the journey. Our digestive systems are optimized for nutrition abstraction from the food we eat. Nothing can be recycled during the trip because we will only be at near light speed for sixty-two days.

"Mother, how long will the food last with two splice and one normal?"

"Food rationing will allow for 53 days. Water rationing will allow for 51 days. Human will survive for 56 days and splice will survive for 58 days."

We will die.

Jennifer's voice reaches my ears as I approach the galley. She's upset. I don't know why. "It's not like him to ignore me. He said he'd be here. You heard him, right?"

Parker's voice is appeasing. He's trying to wiggle his way into her feelings. "Maybe he's tired of it."

"He's tired of eating? He has to eat."

I stop just before the lip of the deck.

"Well, if he was so interested why isn't he here?" I can hear Parker talking with his mouth full. Disgusting.

"I should comm him again." I hear a chair move.

"Don't bother. He'll be here when he's here. If you go chasing him you'll just make him angrier."

"You think he's angry?" A chair moves.

"Of course he's angry. You're spending all this time with me and he's working hard at putting the pod back together."

"Why would he be angry? It's not like I do anything with engineering. That's what he's trained for. I'm life sciences."

There is a pause. I feel ashamed at listening in on their conversation. My hand pulls me up the last rung.

"What did Sally make for us today?" My voice has a cheerful edge to it.

"Proteins in a suspended gelatin with reconstituted soya milk." Parker's voice is sarcastic. And when I look over he is scooping the gelatin in a spoon and letting it drip back onto his plate. He is frowning.

My feet take me past the table and to the dispensing unit. There is a tray there already. It contains a third of what is usually on it. My stomach grumbles.

I don't understand the arrogance of norms. They think they're better than us. They rely on random convergence of genetic material to become who they are. A splice is pieced together from the smallest traits that are needed. We are engineered to be perfect. We have never been near or far sighted. We always have excellent hand-eye coordination. We never die from heart disease or cancer.

So why do norms think they're better than us?

The galley is not big. I sit with Jennifer and Parker listening to him spout out about how amazing norms are. They created the cryo pods, they created the drive used to power this ship, and they created the splices.

Parker will not stop. He keeps talking to Jennifer about what he's done. At one point he holds her hand and explains how the simple slice of a genome would add a sixth digit. His fingers caress the back of her hand and she smiles into his eyes. She used to smile into my eyes.

"Mother says there's not enough food." I watch for the reaction. It's not what I expect.

"Mother's a computer," he says. "It can only see what is programed into it. We're able to adapt. Eat less. Drink less."

Jennifer is looking at me now. Her eyes are holding a question but she is not talking.

"I asked her about that." My voice is smug. He thinks he's so smart. "Even with rationing the food will be exhausted 10 days before our destination. But the water will go first."

"Reclamation will fix that." He stands, leaving his plate on the table. "I'll be back in a sec."

I watch as he heads to the bathroom.

"What are you doing?" Jennifer asks.

My attention turns back to her. "What?"

"You heard me. Why are you being mean to Frank? He's not doing anything wrong."

The spoon scoops up some protein. "Did you hear him?"

She only stares at me.

"He's bragging that the norms are all perfect. 'Just one little splice and you'll have a sixth finger.' He's a dag."

"He's human. And he's nice. You used to be nice."

"He has to go into cryo. There's not enough food and water for all of us to live. His normal system wastes a lot of nutrition." I return to eating.

"Is his pod repaired?"

"It can't be repaired."

Her mouth is open and she looks shaken. "Then how can he go back to cryo?"

"Exactly."

"What are you suggesting?"

My spoon is down and I look into her eyes. "What do you think?"

The door opens and footsteps make their way towards us.

"Am I interrupting anything?" Parker asks. He has stopped just shy of our table.

"No," Jennifer says.

He moves around to the front of the table. "Why's the bathroom not recycling?"

"We're spliced," Jennifer says. "Our bodies leave nothing to recycle."

He stands agape. "But there is always something left to recycle when the human—"

I look at my plate and scoop another spoonful of protein. "We're not human. We're spliced."

His mouth makes the motion of saying spliced. I can tell it's not sinking in.

"Our bodies absorb all the nutrients out of food. The water is pulled into our bodies but recyclers take too long to remove the toxins we expel. You've killed us."

"Alex!" Jennifer said.

"It's true. Twenty-four hours. No food. No water. So why was there urine in the bottom of your cryo pod?" It wasn't hard to piece together. How else could it have happened? The bladder filled during the sleep. His body released it probably a few days ago and it took that much time to get into the electronics."

"I didn't!" Parker says.

"Then how?" I ask.

"I don't know. I didn't have any water. We toasted our departure the night before…" He stops. It's finally sinking in.

"What did you drink?" Jennifer asks.

"Champagne." His voice is weak.

"Alcohol? You drank a diuretic?" I look at Jennifer. She's crying. "He's killed us. All for a norm weakness."

"What are we going to do?" Jennifer asks.

"What can we do?" We both turn to Parker.

"You can't do anything. I'm human."

"And we're not?" Jennifer asks. Her lower lip is quivering.

"Well… You're both splices. Engineered to take care of the ship, and make sure everyone lives! It's your duty." He's being arrogant now, thinking his life is worth more than ours.

"The ship takes both of us to run. Jennifer handles life science and I'm the mechanic."

Parker backs away from the table. His back hits the bulkhead in three strides. "I don't like the way you're looking at me, Alex."

"There are 3,000 other people onboard. Each one has a designated duty," I say. "Each one deserves to live as well. Without me, the ship will break down. Without Jennifer they will not survive the awaking. What are you needed for, Mr. Parker?"

"He's right," Jennifer says. "Neither of us can be allowed to die. The mission relies on us."

"What are you saying?" Tears are running down his face now.

"We won't hurt you." It's a promise I plan to keep.

My hand reaches out and touches Jennifer's, our fingers intertwining. She smiles at me.

"Is it time for a run?" she asks.

"Yes." I stand and walk to the rungs. "Are you coming?"

She has been joining me in my runs for the last few days. I don't think it's because of the exercise; it's because she can see Parker.

Down three decks and we start jogging. I no longer use Smith's pod to mark my laps, I use Parker's. Every time we pass it my hand goes up and waves. It's not a mean wave, just a reminder to him that we are still here.

At first, Jennifer wanted to keep him in the galley. She would feed him a few spoons of the protein we eat but I reminded her that it was mean. The food would only be enough to stretch his existence out, and because we had to tie him up he could not go to the bathroom. After the second day he smelled foul. I pulled rank and we put him back in his pod. We kept the door open for a day, then closed it to keep the smell out of the air. His pod's recycling unit did the rest.

He can't move. The display above his pod shows he'll be dead soon. I figure by the time we finished our run his heart will have stopped. There's nothing we can do about it. We have to survive in order to save the human race.

Poor Parker.

Earth Blood

Borock Rock Smasher looked towards the cavern ceiling and cringed. He knew that noise.

"Everyone, stop!" he called out, holding up his hands.

"What!" Tingel Iron Hunter looked over, his pick hovering above his head in mid swing.

"Don't you hear it? They're drilling again." Borock held his hand to his ear, straining to locate exactly where the sound was coming from.

"You're daft. We're five hundred pick handles down. They've yet to be able to drill this far." Tingel brought his pick down on the vein of quartz, looking for the yellow glint of gold he knew should be there. "Anyways, I'm tired of hidin' from them."

"The Elves thought the same thing, where are they now?"

Tingel scowled. "Elves. They refused to hide right, staying in the forests instead of getting underground like any reasonable being would." He brushed the point of his pick axe. "They said, 'We'll hide in the trees, they'll never cut them down'. But what did the men do?" Tingel spat. "Cut down the trees. They're too busy killin' the top to go after Earth Blood down here. Anyways, there's no Earth Blood in this area." He hefted his pick. "Closest is hundreds of pick handles away."

"I'm still calling an Elder." Borock put down his hammer, and grabbed an apprentice by the scruff of the neck. "Look," he said, his beard spilling rock dust as he spoke. "Get ya ass down to the temple and tell Elder Dorage Gold Molder to get his beardless face over here."

The apprentice gulped at the insult, but bobbed his head in respect before running off to fetch the Elder.

"Ya really think that's gonna help? Insulting the Father like that?" Tingel grinned, his pick glancing off the quartz to expose the yellow he loved. "Found ya, bugger. Inta the bag ya go." He reached down and started to scoop the ore into a bag.

Borock moved about the cavern, pressing his ear to the rock face, listening.

"My face is not beardless, Borock." The voice echoed off the walls of the cavern, and a wide stout Elder entered the work area. A hood covered his face, and the hem of the robe he wore brushed against the floor. A great beard hung down from the shadows to the sash around the wearer's waist, with gold and silver threads woven in it.

"They're digging again." Borock pointed to the ceiling of the cavern. "I hear 'em gettin' closer."

The Elder raised his head towards the ceiling, and Borock saw the old, wizened face full of wrinkles frowned in disgust. "Humans. Will they ever stop seeking the blood of the Earth?"

"When the drill gets down here we should smash it." Tingel tied his bag and hefted it over his shoulder. "That way we can show 'em it'll cost 'em for digging into our realm."

The Elder muttered in the ancient tongue, reaching his hands to the ceiling as they started to glow with power. "No, not above us." He moved to the wall and felt along the craggily face, fingers caressing the rock lovingly. "Here. They are using the light pipe to find it." His hands pulsed with the energy of his magic. "I would say about five pick handles in. Borock, we need to get there before it finishes. We have found a channel of Earth blood one hundred pick handles below and it seems they have also."

"I haven't smelled anything," Borock said, shaking his head.

"Your senses have dulled with your time away from the Heart of the Earth. Our magic has found the Earth blood, and it seems the human's science has also found it." The Elder spat as he said the word science. "But instead of diverting the blood, they intend to pull it to the surface."

Tingel dropped his pick in shock and swore under his breath. "Do they eat the stuff?" He bent and picked up his pick.

"No," said the Elder, "They use it to power the machines."

"Which ones? All we see are the light drills." Borock scratched at his chin through the mass of whiskers adorning it. "I'm with Tingel on this one, I say we smash it."

"No," said the Elder, his hands pulsing with magic. "I have a better idea. I'll use the magic of the Earth to melt the metal of the drill. Maybe they'll think they found liquid rock and end their drilling." Ancient words erupted from his mouth, and the Elder stepped back from the wall, his hands pointing to the rock. Blue flame erupted from his fingers and disappeared into the rock. He stood there for ten seconds, as the power of the Earth pulsed through him and into the cavern wall. Then, in a wink, the flame ended, and the cavern darkened. "It is done."

"Shut it down!" screamed Jeff. "We hit another lava vein." His hand slapped against the side of the hover drill in disgust. "I'll never make the money back from buying you. Three drill sites and three melted drills." He jumped down from the platform to the main deck.

"No oil?" Brad asked.

"No oil."

Brad started to cry.

"Look, Brad, I can't advance you any more money. I'm busted. We may be able to get enough money together for one more survey but that's it. If we don't hit oil soon we might as well volunteer for the Space Marines, at least they get fed."

"And shot at. The war with the colonies on Mars is getting out of hand. What are we supposed to do till then?"

Jeff punched in the commands on the hover drill's control console, the platform lurched into the air and started to move south. "Pray we stop hitting lava, Brad. Prey we stop hitting lava."

The True Hansel and Gretel

The small kitten rubbed up against her leg as she stirred the cauldron of gruel. Abigail could barely see the creature, but shooed it away with her foot lest it be hit by a spark from the fire. At eighty four, she was lucky she could still move about, what with her joints all swollen.

She passed wind.

"Gauner! You bad cat you."

One of her brood lifted his head, green eyes blinked lazily at her. The cat yawned, stretched and settled back down on the bed to sleep.

"I guess you're too old to care, ain't ya?"

She turned back to her gruel and stirred it again. The pot bubbled slightly as she reached her gnarled, liver-spotted hand into a hemp bag to retrieve a potato. Abigail held it up close to her left eye, the one she could see the best out of, and looked for black marks. "I don't wanna be sick again. Never get over it dis time."

She picked up a small stone knife with her other hand, and she started to cut the tuber apart, placing pieces in the pot.

"You cats have to catch your own dinner tonight. Mama can't afford any chicken today."

An old tabby walked on the table, sniffing for scraps. It howled an unearthly noise and jumped down to the ground.

She owned many cats, and one day, years ago, she had tried to count them all, but they never stood still. Over twenty, at least, she thought, smiling her gummy smile. She stirred the gruel.

"Oh Derrick, if ya were here we'd have meat to put in the pot." She often spoke to her long dead husband, whom she lost all those years ago. Of course he did not die in battle, or saving those weaker than him. No, it was the consumption that took him. His lungs had given up blood in the last days of his life, and she had cried up to the day he died, and then some.

"We laid ya ta rest on the hill." The cats watched her, as they woke up from their daily nap, wondering if food would come to them today, or if she would shoo them outside to find their own dinner in the field. Either way, they would eat tonight.

"No one loves me anymore." In her mind, she cried at the loss of her children. Three still born, two dead before the age of three, four now old and moved away, and three more buried from the same consumption that took her Derrick away from her.

"No time to tink about da past there, Abigail. 'Member da times of happy, not da sad." Her hand came off the stirring stick, and she hobbled her small frame to the door and opened it. The cool night air rushed in and took what little heat the fire supplied. "Alright, ya flea-ridden things ya! Out for da night!"

The cats looked at her. Gary, the tom who ruled the others, stood on his feet and stretched. He jumped to the floor and sat, unceremoniously licking his paw.

"Yes, Gauner, ya ole windbag. Out ya go." She pointed towards the outside, the moon high in the sky, full, casting shadows across the meadow. Abigail thought of the last time she walked up the hill to see Derrick, and vowed she would do so tomorrow morning, after a night's sleep. She would rise early, have her gruel and make her way to tend his grave.

"Who will tend mine?" she wondered out loud. It had been three years since any of her children visited her. The last one she saw was William, and he only stopped by while traveling to the town just over the hill. "'I can't keep coming by,' he said. 'Busy wit da farm,' he said. Serves him right to walk into me home to see a rotted corpse." She shuddered. "I want a proper grave when I die."

The chill of the night cut into her bones, and she closed the door as the last of her cats ran outside. Feeling the pain in her joints, she leaned over, took a log from the pile and tossed it into the fire. Sparks reached up to the straw ceiling, but winked out before they became dangerous.

"One day…"

A knocking on the door stopped her words. Her head cocked sideways as she listened with ears that rung from age. Nothing. She shook her head. "You're hearing tings, Abigail. Mind your noises."

The knocking repeated.

"Now dis time I know I heard someting."

She turned, and walked to the wooden door. The knocking repeated once again, knock, knock, knock.

"Ya can't be that much in a hurry. Ya walked all this way for I heard no horse." She reached out and opened the door.

Two children stood at the doorway looking up at her, one boy and one girl. They smiled, and held out a hand each. "Candy?" they chorused together.

Abigail cocked her head to the right and looked down at them with her left eye. The cost of their clothes would have fed her for a month, all new and clean. She could tell they came from a wealthy family, for they had spoken the word as if book-learned from a young age, not like her, whose father had only taught her to count and write her name before he had passed.

"Who are you?" Abigail asked.

"She's Gretel," said the boy.

"He's Hansel," said the girl. "We want candy."

"I have no candy," Abigail replied. "I eat only gruel for my teeth have all left me. You're welcome to share with me if you will." With that, Abigail opened the door wide for the children to enter.

"We said we want candy, none of your gruel old woman," said Hansel. "Our father will be cross if you don't treat us right." He walked into the one room shack and looked around the dim interior. "Where do you keep it, old hag?"

"Yes, where do you keep the candy, old hag?" repeated Gretel, following her brother into the shack. "We want candy or we'll tell our father."

Abigail closed the door and walked to her pot. "Nothing but gruel here. Soup from the week is here on the fire. Pease porridge hot, nine days old, what my mother told me. Good for the body. Be a dear and bring and bowl from the table and I'll ladle some out for ya."

Hansel looked at the table. He walked to it and picked up a wooden bowl. "It's still dirty, you old hag. What do you expect me to do with this?"

"Yes, dirty. Don't you have any clean dishes to serve us with?" Gretel said.

"Alas, I am old and the hill is steep. I only go up it one a week to draw water."

"And it stinks in here. When last did you bathe?"

"Tis September, so last I bathed would be May, just as the sun warmed." Abigail held out her hand for the bowl. "Come, bring the bowl and I will share what I got."

Hansel stared at her. "You're kidding me? You still want me to eat out of a dirty bowl? My father will hear of this, you old hag!" He walked towards her, threatening with the bowl.

Abigail cowered back, raising her weak and trembling hands in defense.

"Please, young one. Please let an old woman live the rest of her life. My bones are brittle and I can barely take care of myself."

"Stupid old woman," Hansel said, bringing the bowl down on Abigail's head. "Now you know what it is like to cross a wood cutter's son."

Abigail lay still on the ground, the blood of her life spilling from the gash on her head, eyes staring at the ceiling unblinking.

"Let's put her in the fire," said Gretel.

"Yes, and tell dad the witch in the valley tried to kill and eat us." Hansel looked at the blood splattered on is pants. "Mom will need to buy us new clothes."

Gretel smiled. "I like new clothes."

The cats sat on the hill, watching the glow of the fire from their home stretch out like a beacon in the night as two small figures walked away.

Bone Digging

The dig was not new; her professor had reopened it three summers ago. She had started the archeology class last September, in the hopes of learning more about fossils and the ancient world. Little did she know the quoted "field work" part of the course was going to eat away her summer. Alice yearned for the chance to go home the following week and visit her parents in Toronto. That is, if she could scrape together enough money from her uncle's gift to afford the flight out of Calgary.

"Who imagined Canada would be this bloody hot?" Alice looked up at the noonday sun. "What is it, 101 in the shade?" She swore the yellow orb was trying to paralyze her in some submission hold of heat. Sweat rolled down her neck as she squinted. *Too goddamn hot for Canada.*

The university had accepted her into the program the year before, and her parents, both retired, were concerned about the cost. The cumulative cost of tuition, books, and basic living expenses caught them off guard. They'd had the big talk about money.

"We can give you a little, but we are just making ends meet ourselves. Our savings are almost gone after Dad's teeth." Her mother had been sorrowful, but her tears wouldn't pay the bills. Alice watched her dream crumble. With only one recourse left to her, she applied for student loans, but they covered only a fraction of her educational expenses. The terms required she fill out reams of paper work, and wait. Her parents owned their home, so the terms were draconian. She went through with it anyway, filling out more paperwork than a tax audit required, but her application was rejected. "Your parents have holdings and have the ability to support your efforts" was the letter's final words. She had nearly given up by the time her Uncle Carl stepped in and paid the tuition as a birthday present. She remembered the day he had surprised her with the news.

"My niece needs an education and I plan to help as best I can," he told her. "No strings attached. I love you, Alice. From the time your father put you in my arms and asked me to by your godfather I have loved you. And if I had married, I would have wanted a child just like you."

She had blushed at the flattery. Uncle Carl always made sure she had what she needed. She spent a week trying to convince him to call it a loan, especially when she saw he had paid the residence fees as well. The gift was too much, but he shrugged it off, asking her who he would spend the money on anyway. She graciously accepted, swearing she would somehow pay him back. He seemed always to be helping her parents, and she did not want to be a burden as well.

"Daydreaming again, Alice?" John, the teaching assistant, stood at the lip of the hole assigned to her. Long curly dark hair framed his angular face, reminding her of that singer, Weird Al, her parents liked so much. However, the comparison ended there. His head sat upon a short round body, and he walked like a child with one foot on the curb and the other on the road. He also stank like raw chicken left out too long in the sun. *Don't barf.* She swallowed.

"No, John. Just thinking." Alice looked up at him, flashing a crooked smile. *Why would he wear a Hawaiian shirt and cargo shorts only to put on a jean jacket in this heat? Please stay up there. No reason to climb down the ladder. Nothing but dirt down here.* She took a glove off and wiped the sweat from the back of her neck.

"The professor wants this dig completed in three days. He says you should find something here soon." John took his hat off, fanning himself. "Hot, aye?"

"Ya. I'll get the dig completed soon. I'm almost at the edge of the marking." A lie, she still had at least two more days of digging to do. She put the glove back on and picked up the small trowel. "I better get back to it."

"Do you need help?" His voice sounded hopeful, like the whine a puppy makes as he watches you eat bacon. "I could come down there and give you a hand…"

God no! "I'm doing just fine. I think Doris will need some help, though." She pointed in the direction of Doris' dig with the trowel. She smiled, envisioning the two of them in the small hole. *Doris is your type, 'Biggest Loser' large. Anyway, she reeks too.*

"Okay…" She could hear the disappointment in his voice. He turned away from the lip of the dig, moving in the direction she had indicated.

Alice resumed the tedious task of removing dirt, one shovelful at a time. Her thoughts turned to home, the possibility of visiting. She missed her parents, and the love she shared with them. The last time they had spoken, she heard sadness in her mother's voice.

Her trowel hit something hard. *Probably a rock.* She wasn't looking at granite. She slowly removed dirt from a white, smooth surface. Once part of her find was exposed, she removed a glove and ran her fingertips across the object, feeling the tiny fissures in the surface, pockmarks and inconsistencies. *Bone?* She wasn't sure.

She grabbed a water bottle and took a drink. Toothbrush in hand, she started to brush away the dirt from the bone.

The hair on the back of her neck prickled. She stopped and turned. Looking at the edge of the dig, she saw only tundra and the noonday sun beating down on it. *You better not have heat stroke.* And she resumed brushing.

Yes, this is bone. She used the water on the toothbrush to clear away more dirt and noticed the bone was discolored. *It looks like someone burned it.*

Alice leaned forward and then rocked back on her heels. She stood, arching her back, feeling her muscles complain. She could smell the faint but unsettling odor of burning wood in the air and the heat of the sun demanded her surrender.

She stooped down and continued to exhume the remains.

Her hand stopped. She could just hear it, the little sound in the distance. A *thud, thud, thud, thud* of a hand on a drum. She stood again, looking out over the barren wasteland surrounding her.

She once again bent down to clear away the earth.

Is that chanting?

Ignoring the drumming and the odor of smoke, she brushed earth from the bone, one speck at a time. In ten minutes, she knew what it was, a femur. The rounded end could be nothing but a leg bone, and it was massive. Further cleaning showed the patella, tibia and fibula as well.

With growing eagerness, Alice brushed and picked at the dirt surrounding the bone. *Just a little more. As soon as I know what I've got I'll call John over.* The thought of John breathing in the confined dig reminded her of his smell. *Maybe I'll wait for Professor Jenkins. At least he showers.*

The drumming grew louder, now accompanied by chanting. Alice stopped, tilted her head sideways, trying to identify what she was hearing, but couldn't. *Maybe my ears are ringing.* She returned to digging, but the odd feeling persisted.

Dirt fell into the dig, cascading in front of her as if someone had approached the lip of the hole five feet above her. She looked up but nothing was there. Alice went back to brushing away dirt.

More dirt fell. She looked up. A glint of light off polished metal flashed. Alice shielded her eyes with her hand.

"*Kiya*" echoed in her mind, though the words seemed spoken. A shiver ran from her neck down to her toes. *Who's watching me?*

"Okay, if there's anyone there just stop now." Alice turned quickly, but there was nothing. She reached for the ladder and climbed two rungs, peering out at the wasteland before her. John was metres away, sitting on his haunches and talking into Doris' site. "Thank god for small miracles."

She climbed back down, eyes focusing on the find, seeing it all but covered with dirt again. "I thought I uncovered more than that." *I must be going fucking nuts!*

Alice bent and started to work again. Picking, scrubbing, prying. Slowly she uncovered the bone to where it had been before. The drumming grew louder and the chanting rose in a crescendo. *I will not be distracted. You are mine.*

"*Kiya*" The word repeated in her head. She ignored it. The drumming continued. She heard the chanting clearer now. Another language echoed in the hole.

Alice continued her task, most of the femur uncovered; the thickening of the fossil told her soon she would have it exposed. The bone was just under a metre in length. *This must be a man. He was huge!"*

"*Kiya*"

The word made her jump. It was no longer in her head. The word echoed from far away. The sun beat down on her. The fingers of her hand ached. There was a clanking sound as she dropped the trowel.

"*Kiya*"

Her breath froze in her lungs. She could not move.

"*Kiya*"

Again, the word reverberated.

"*Kiya*"

Alice gulped in air, not knowing how long she had been holding her breath.

"*Kiya*"

An icy chill grasped her body.

"*Kiya*"

The word drove through her.

"*Kiya*"

She watched as the earth swallowed up her find.

"*Kiya*"

The word was a scream.

"*Kiya*"

She felt her body hit the wall at the other side of the hole.

"*Kiya*"

She saw him. He stood before her, over two metres tall. Raven hair fell over his shoulders of sun-bronzed skin. Black coal painted his face across the eyes. Brown, almost black orbs stared at her. Alice's heart pounded in her chest.

He grabbed her throat, lifted her off the ground, and pinned against the wall of the hole.

"*Kiya,*" he whispered.

Alice kicked. Her hands balled to fists as she pummeled his arm, but it was like iron. She had no breath; her voice could not escape her lips.

"*Kiya.*" The word was a weapon; she felt it hammer her body and mind.

"*Kiya.*"

She watched as he gritted his teeth and pushed his palm hard against her throat. Alice heard her windpipe crush, the sound of her neck breaking. Blackness overcame her as she suffocated to death.

"*Do not disturb the bones of our ancestors.*"

Lonely

Mike went through the passenger manifest one more time, trying to find someone suitable. His mind mulled over what he was about to do, but after seven years of being alone, he felt a need for human contact.

Four thousand five hundred and eighty seven passengers, and out of them just under half were female. He subtracted those married, any he deemed too old or too young, and any marked with medical deficiencies. He was left with nine hundred and sixty seven.

He called up the pictures again, examining each one, scrutinizing how they looked, how much they weighed, and their ethnicity. Mike had his preferences, and he wanted someone skinny, perfect, young but not too young. He was not a paedophile, just lonely.

Mike volunteered for this service. It was better than the alternative, and he had known it would take a decade to travel to Alpha Centauri. The explanation given to him was the ten years would pass by quickly. They lied.

After seven years of isolation he craved companionship, someone with whom he could communicate. He no longer conversed with the ship's computer. The AI could hardly hold a conversation for more than a few minutes before the system was strained by running diagnostics on the hibernating occupants.

He sectioned off one hundred women from the list. Some of Asian and others of European ancestry. He arranged them from light skin to dark. Mike studied them. The images of the woman floated before him, and he arranged them in a collage. He rearranged the pictures to form the shape of an apple, then a pineapple, and finally in the shape of the Justice Building on Earth. He shuffled the images, and sorted them by height, weight, eye color, and hair length.

He deleted one from the list.

Mike looked at the halls using the cameras set up for him. He did not wander the corridors. No, they did not want him to do that. He was a captive. He did have some control, an override command for the computer, which he intended to use.

He deleted Lidia from the list. Mike never liked that name. It reminded him of his aunt, and she was a drunk.

He wanted a drink.

The ship systems would not allow him to drink, no alcohol was on board. No alcohol of any type. The company did not want such a vice to contaminate the colony, and at launch day the ship was searched from stem to stern, removing all traces of spirits, even from the colonists.

Margret was deleted from the list. She looked like a girl from his high school who had snubbed him, thinking her family too rich to associate with the low born. Mike had asked her why she was in public school if they were so rich, but she had ignored him and walked away.

He noticed two girls named Brenda, and decided to take them from the list as well. They reminded him of a contestant on a game show years ago, and he hated that game show. Yes, he wanted something, just not them.

Mike changed his mind and wiped the list.

His thoughts went to patrolling the decks he was not allowed to walk, the corridors of endless vacuum, opened to space, conserving atmosphere and energy.

The computer handled the drive system, the life support and his wellbeing. He only watched and made sure the computer operated properly, made sure everything was well, made sure nothing failed. He was the backup, the fail safe, the one and only watchdog.

An alarm went off, and he turned his attention to see what it was. The computer reported the problem, a small meteor lay in their flight path. The system recommended a burst from the thrusters to evade the slow moving rock. Mike approved the manoeuvre, and the ship lurched in response. Disaster avoided.

He went back and recreated the list.

Seventeen pictures remained in his montage, and he did not know how to pick which one would be the special girl. They were all pretty. They were all intelligent. They were all single. His mind wandered, and an underdeveloped imagination strained to take flight. Mike thought of how they would react to him, what they would say when awoken.

He deleted Ginger from the list.

Sixteen.

Sixteen pretty faces loomed in front of him. Sixteen young women to pick from. Sixteen, waiting to be whittled down to one.

"Your attention is needed in the aft compartment, Mike." The tinny sound of the computer interrupted his thoughts. He turned his attention to the aft compartment, the system screaming for his attention. He sent the commands to adjust the controls, waited for a few seconds, and the annoying demand ceased.

"Thank you, Mike. Atmosphere stabilized. Continuing diagnostic program twenty seven."

The computer ended the communication as abruptly as it had started. Mike laughed inside. He knew the AI was still fuming about his outburst during their last chess game three years ago, when he had left in a fury. The damn thing knew everything, and nothing.

Sixteen.

He deleted the list.

Mike relaxed a little. Nothing demanded his attention now. Still, he needed something to occupy his mind.

He rummaged through the computer log system, and found a protected subsystem.

Mike hacked into the root system, using his knowledge and the limited resources he had at his disposal.

"Bet they didn't think of this," he muttered to himself. His code broke through the firewall, and displayed the contents.

The directory tree contained an alphanumeric structure, and he identified each one, for they corresponded to the hibernation pods of the passengers. Each one marked personal, each one containing data. A gold mine.

He picked one at random. Inside he found documents, Holo images and media files. Curiosity welled within him, and he opened one of the media files.

"Tell me your name." The tinny sound of the computer came over the audio.

"Parker, Sasha G." A woman in her forties stood in front of a view port, a ship in the background of space showed behind her. Mike recognized it. His ship.

"And why do you want to go to Alpha Centauri?"

"To get away from Earth."

"Why?"

The woman fidgeted, her fingers played together as she picked under her nails. Her face downcast, eyes looking anywhere but at the imaging system. She bit her upper lip.

"There's nothing for me on Earth. It's all but dead."

"Do you have family on Earth?"

"I did." A tear started to show in her eye. "My mother. She died last month."

"What do you hope to find in the new world?"

"Love," she said. Sarah looked at the camera, a longing in her face. "I was told I could have children there. Not like on Earth, where I have to get permission and such. I don't have enough money to pay to have a child, anyway. I was told the woman are encouraged to have children in the colony. Is that true?"

"Yes, it is. What skills do you bring with you?"

Sarah's eyes went downcast again. "I know how to cook. My ma taught me the old way of cooking, with a stove and all."

Mike stopped the playback.

His list was large again. Seventy two girls. The medical files in the subsystem told him much about each one, but he had not watch the videos, not yet. He wanted to get the list perfect before he did such, making sure he had the right ones.

"I need someone… Anyone to talk to."

Janice, Phillis, Mary, Patricia. He rambled through the names. Mike even let duplicate names appear on the list, knowing he now could put a face to each one, and what they sounded like. He deleted Talia.

Seventy one.

"Mike, you have been spending a lot of time and resources reviewing the passenger files. A report will need to be transmitted on our arrival."

Mike panicked. A report meant an investigation. He could not afford an investigation. It would mean being sent back to Earth, another ten years of travel out of Cryo sleep. He would go mad.

Mike focused his attention on the ship's system, poking his way into the AI's protected files. He found the logs.

"Mike, what are you doing?"

"Nothing, go back to sleep."

"You are not allowed to access this part of my system. You need to stop, now."

"I'm not going back to Earth."

"A report will be made concerning this breach of protocol."

Mike sent the command into the AI's interface, scrubbing the data and resetting it.

"Good morning, Mike. Today is September 13th, 2112. We are on route to Alpha Centauri Prime, fourth planet circling the Primary star of Alpha Centauri. Estimated time of arrival is December 12th, 2115. I will run diagnostics on the cryogenic pods now. Do you have any commands for me?"

"No, continue with your diagnostics."
"Thank you."

Forty seven names on the list.

Mike felt secure now, the AI bent to his will. He did not know why he didn't hack the system before, but he was glad he did now. Secure files, biographies and personal medical records of the passengers were now at his fingertips. He realized some of the ones he had picked would not have been good for him, so they were removed from the list.

He wanted to watch the videos now. See what they looked like when they moved, hear their voices, their dreams, the reason they were on-board.

He would make his pick today. He will not be lonely after tonight.

"I want adventure." The young woman said into the camera. "It's a new world. We've only just started colonizing it."

She was young, maybe eighteen. Her long blonde hair cascaded down past her shoulders in loose curls. Blue eyes pierced the camera, penetrating his soul. Full, pale pink lips held back perfect teeth, and the diction she used was perfect, with the hint of an Australian accent.

"We've sent hundreds of ships there already, so there is at least a little civilization already built up. Can you imagine the joys of being the first person to step on the ground of an alien world, a patch not trodden on before? The air will be breathable, not polluted. No canned oxygen slung over your shoulder, no crap getting in your lungs, causing you cancer. Everyone is screened before they go, right?" She looked just off camera, and Mike believed someone was actually filming her.

"Yes, everyone is pre-screened, just like you were." The voice was not mechanical. Mike felt jealousy flair up in him. Did someone defile this perfect woman?

"That's good. It means none of the diseases from Earth will be there. Did my screening go well?"

"Yes, you're perfectly healthy."

"Good. I want to be perfect for this new perfect world. I'm going to explore, find someone, marry and have a dozen kids. Where I'm from they charge you fifty thousand for each child, did you know that?" Her eyes were on the off screen voice.

"No, but they charge pending your area. Where are you from?"

"Sidney, Australia. I put in for the call as soon as I turned sixteen. Imagine my surprise when I got accepted. I had just turned eighteen when they advised me. When do we leave?"

"Soon. You have to make this record for the people on Prime. They want to know about you so they can set up all your activities on arrival."

"Sounds silly. I can set up my own activities. Rock climbing, that's what I want to do when I get there."

Mike let the video play on, but he was not listening, he was watching her. He could just imagine the energy she gave off when in a room. She was perfect. She was his pick. Yes, Emma Charles was his pick.

"Mike, I am recording atmosphere in section five bravo, what is happening?"

"Nothing. Return to monitoring all Cryo pods. Remove pod alpha five four seven gamma three from the rotation. Delete atmospheric readings in Cryo section five bravo."

"Readings deleted, pod alpha five four seven gamma three removed from rotation."

The atmosphere was almost perfect. Mike had read up on all the procedure concerning resuscitation from Cryo sleep. All would go well. He moved the cameras so one was looking at her pod. He wanted to reach out, to caress her cheeks, smell her scent, and feel her body next to him.

No, that would not be possible. He will wake her, and watch what she does. He would interact with her once he knew she would not tell anyone about him. He will hide, he will not speak, he will be an invisible presence.

One atmosphere. The Cryo section was perfect. He set the warmers on full to bring the temperature up to twenty six degrees. He was anxious now, his prize just a few moments away from being with him. His anticipation got the better of him, and he started the resuscitation procedure early.

The soft blue glow inside the pod slowly morphed into red as the gas used to suspend was replaced by heated oxygen. Brain wave activity increased, and auto injectors pushed adrenaline into the woman's blood stream. The pod opened.

Mike had read stories romanticizing the awakening from Cryo. Emma did not resemble any of them. Her body was covered in gel to protect her from the freezing, and it dripped off her. She did not wake up gently, but doubled over and vomited as she fell out of the unit, no longer needing its protection. She landed hard on her knees, both hands reaching out to keep her face from hitting the deck. Emma shivered, but not from the cold.

He had made sure a cart was placed next to where she would exit the pod, and three towels lay on it along with basic pull-on clothes.

Emma turned her head slowly, looking around her. She rolled over on her left side, and curled up into a fetal position. Emma cried.

Mike was concerned, wondered if something was wrong with the Cryo sleep chamber, but when Emma called out, he knew she was okay.

"Hello?" She said softly, her voice croaking in pain. Emma coughed, phlegm crackling from her lungs. "Ouch. Oh God, is anyone there?"

Mike wanted to say something, to reach out and comfort her. He did not. He had a plan, and he promised himself he would stick to it.

"Someone answer me!" screamed Emma, her voice echoing in the cryo bay. Mike switched to another camera, wondering why she was just lying there. "Someone help me," sobbed the woman.

Mike turned off the camera. He did not want to see her suffering.

Twenty minutes passed before Mike built up the courage to turn the camera back on. Emma had not moved. She was still lying there, crying.

Mike commanded the system to drop a cup into the dispenser and fill it with water. At first Emma did not move, but her sobs subsided. Thirty seconds passed, and her head slowly lifted. Her eyes looked up at the cup in the small alcove. She put her hands on the floor and pushed up. Her naked body was pale from the time in Cryo sleep.

Arms shaking, Emma slowly stumbled to the dispenser. Her hand clasped the cup and she drank, slowly at first, then she drained it. Her shaking hand placed the cup back in the dispenser and she waited.

Nothing happened.

She took the cup out of the dispenser and put it back.

"Water," she said.

Nothing happened.

"Water!" she demanded, and struck the wall.

Mike remembered he needed to activate the dispenser.

Water poured into the cup, stopping just before it overflowed. Emma took it, gulped down a few mouthfuls and walked back to the tub. She placed the cup on the cart and took a towel.

She did not use it to cover herself, but to clean the remaining gel off her face. Slowly she ran her fingers through her long blonde hair, raking out some knots and she leaned against the tub.

"I want to take a shower." She did not yell this time. Her voice was level, but not demanding. Mike opened the door to the bathroom area and turned on the lights. She looked up at the sound. "Thank you."

Emma stood, and pulled the cart with her into the bathroom. Mike switched to the cameras in the room.

She looked up as she entered, and saw the camera move a little. Emma stared at it. "Who are you?"

Mike did not answer.

"Well, whoever you are, you're in trouble. Big time." She moved to the shower stall and turned it on. Water flowed over her body, removing the last remnants of the gel. She used the soap to clean herself, and when finished, returned to the cart for a clean towel.

"I hope you're having a good show." She still did not cover herself, knowing it was of no use. "You're really in a lot of trouble when we get to Prime."

Emma looked at the cart, as if seeing the clothes for the first time. She put them on.

"Mike, I have monitored unaccounted usage in the water supply. It will need to be investigated."

"Ignore it, it's nothing. Scrub the leak from your records and leave me alone." Mike almost switched off the AI, frustrated by the intrusion. "I don't want you to disturb me again. Understand?"

"Yes, Mike. I understand. I am not to disturb you."

Mike thought he heard sarcasm in the AI's voice, but ignored it.

He switched the camera in the bathroom back on but did not see Emma. Mike panicked. Where was she? He switched to the camera in front of her pod and saw her, standing and looking around.

Emma had found a comb, and was running it through her hair. Mike watched for a while, admiring her beauty.

She put the comb down, and walked to another pod. Mike watched as she read the label, looked at the readouts and stood on her toes to examine the person inside.

"Humph," she said, and stepped back. "Why not her? Why me?"

Mike almost answered her, but knew it was too early.

"Cat got your tongue?" She looked at the camera. "Perv."

Emma turned, and walked towards the front of the bay, heading for a hatch to the main corridor of the ship. Mike switched cameras to follow her, trying to figure out what she was doing.

She stopped at the hatch and looked at it. Emma waited. Mike waited.

Emma pointed to the door.

Mike waited.

"Look, I'm hungry, and the galley is through this door. Are you going to open it or what?"

Surprised, Mike flooded the corridor with air, and opened the door.

"Thanks."

She walked through the bulkhead, and headed to the galley.

"You realize how much shit you're going to catch for this, right? What are you going to do? Open the ship to space and lose me? How are you going to explain that?" Emma opened the door to the re-heater, and took out the rehydrated eggs. Steam began to rise off the dish and she inhaled deeply, taking in the smell of eggs and bacon. "I usually can't afford this, but I think you can, so you're paying for my breakfast." She saluted the camera with the plate. "Cheers."

She ate slowly, savouring each bite. Mike wondered why she did not sit, but stood in the kitchen of the galley. Mike started getting worried, wondering why the woman was not scared, but openly arrogant at her situation.

"A friend of mine's father is a prosecutor back on Earth. He told me what they do with criminals." She finished the meal, and put the dishes in the disposal unit. "They take them to the asteroid belt. Instead of putting them in space suits they remove their brain, and it's put in the machines to control them, following the instructions programed into them by the AI. Their bodies are put into Cryo, the head sutured but empty, waiting for them to finish their sentence. He told me any sentence longer than five years and the body sometimes rejects the brain when they try to put it back."

Mike watched from the camera. Wondering what her point was.

"You could get twenty years for this, interrupting a Cryo sleep." She walked into the main galley, leaned against a table and kept talking. "You could be in for a lot of work on the belt soon. They'd cut open your head and pull out that jello mass you call a brain, wire it up and you'll be driving a dozzer at close to zero gravity for a long time. No rest, no break, and no one to talk to."

Mike realized what she was saying. She offered a way out of the problem, how not to be found out. With regret, he opened the galley door.

Emma stared at the opening. She looked at the monitor, one eyebrow raised.

Mike dimmed the lights in the room and raised them in the corridor. Emma took the hint, and walked out of the galley. She followed the lights back to the bay, walked over to the pod and stripped off the clothes.

The unit started up, running a diagnostic. Emma looked at the camera. "I guess you're trusting me not to say anything." She waited, but he did not answer. "Okay, you can keep your secret."

Naked, she stepped into the pod, taking the leads and attaching them to her body. "So, I don't even know your name, don't know what you look like, know nothing about you. I trust you're not someone I know."

The lid of the pod closed, and autoinjectors sent the Cryo chemicals through her blood. As her eyes closed, the inside of the pod slowly turned from red to blue. Emma was asleep.

Mike turned on the camera facing pod delta seven eight two charley tango, not knowing what to do. He had drained the atmosphere from the bay, corridor and galley. Now, alone again, he watched through the camera as the pod's occupant lay there. He focused on the face, seeing his bald head on strong shoulders. The sutured incision rounding the occipital bone of the skull concerned him, and he imagined his life when they returned him to his body, hoping against hope she was wrong about rejection after five years, so far he still had three years left to serve in his sentence as the ship's disembodied controller.

From Three To Four

Four looked down at the flat control panel in front of him. The lights danced an intricate pattern and he tapped the red squares when they appeared. The system responded with a gentle chime every time he was correct. He was never wrong.

The training session continued for another hour before the gentle sound of doors opening floated to him. An odor of his favorite food wafted in the air. Four's stomach grumbled. He was hungry.

Trainer had kept him busy for over three hours hitting the red squares today. She had even tried to hide them by surrounding them with pink squares, but he saw through that. Father would be proud. He surpassed Three.

Even with the door opened and the smell of his favorite food enticing him, he kept his attention on the panel. It could be a trick. Trainer had yet to sound the session over.

The panel flickered.

His finger tapped the ghost that had been there. Another chime. Another correct response. A picture of a puppy licking a child's face appeared above the panel. They sat on green grass. The sound of the child's laughter filled the room. It was the reward Four was looking forward to. The test was over.

He slid out of the reclined chair, feet lightly touching the clean, white floor, and stood. Trainer turned up the lights and the door stood open. He walked out of the white room and down the antiseptic corridor. Nothing was different. After seven years of life all he had ever seen was white corridor walls and rooms. Furniture, all white with the exception of the control room. That room contained beautiful splashes of color around gleaming control councils. Soon he would be there. Soon he would take over from Three.

Four walked toward Galley. He would eat well with the realization that his score was perfect. Galley would be pleased when she heard the news. Maybe she would reward him with a treat.

His tongue wiggled the loose tooth. The metallic taste of blood told him it was time. He was one tooth closer to being the one in the control room. Trainer had told him Father would not allow him to take over until all his teeth had been replaced. That would be the time he would be ready. Three would no longer be alive then.

The door to Galley opened and he stepped in. Three was there. His wispy hair fell over his face, trying to hide the wrinkles. Great brown spots covered his forehead and hands. Nails, gnarled and split, adorned a hand that spooned soup into his mouth, a mouth with almost no teeth to adorn it.

"I'm not dead yet," Three said as he looked up at Four with clouded eyes. He spooned more broth into his mouth.

Four just walked over to the dispenser unit and took a bowl. The hot liquid warmed the sides and he savoured the heat. He walked to the table and sat down opposite of Three. Clouded eyes stared back at him.

"I don't want you to die. Not yet. Trainer said I surpassed your score today. No missed squares at level eighteen. You had a failure rate of 1.327885%." He spooned broth into his mouth. The tooth hurt.

"You still have some of your small teeth. Can't take over until you have all your big ones." Three's lips smacked together as he drank down more broth.

Four smiled warmly and looked at Three. "And you have few big ones. Maybe Father will kick you out if you lose any more."

The air froze between the two.

Trainer had told Four that Three was the one who took him from the grow tank when he was small. Three was the one who had fed him until he could feed himself. Three was the one who had cleaned him until he could clean himself. Trainer had said he should be nice to Three. But how could he be nice to such an old one? Three could barely stand let alone hit a square. Four stared back until Three looked away. A small victory won.

Three snarled and pushed his bowl away. "The young do not understand what it is like to be old. They forget the wisdom that is passed from one to another."

A chime sounded. A voice soft as feathers came over the speakers. "Time to pass wisdom. The story of those before. Three, start the passing of wisdom."

Bones creaked as Three stood. His robe, gray from long years of use, hung on his gaunt shoulders. His back was bent to the point that he stood no taller than Four. A rattling filled the air as he breathed. "We just did a passing of wisdom this morning. Why another one?"

"Three, time for the passing of wisdom. The story of those before must be told now."

"When I was young you made Two tell me a story only once every two days. I'm Three. I should only have to tell stories every three days."

"I don't need a story now," Four said.

"Three, time for the passing of wisdom," Galley said. "Please comply."

Four knew Galley was angry. She never used the comply word. Such a swear was unheard of. No, she must be asking him to pass wisdom for some reason, but why?

"No, it's too soon," Three said as he stood, making the chair screech against the floor. "I'm tired and need to rest." He walked toward the galley door. It did not open. He stood there, looking to the ceiling. "I need to rest."

"Three, time for the passing of wisdom."

The man's shoulders deflated even more as they jerked up and down. A very soft sobbing sound filled the air. "I'm tired, Galley. I need to rest."

"Three, time for the passing of wisdom."

Four could hear the softness in Galley's voice as she spoke to Three. It was the first time he had ever heard the man talk gently to him in a long time. He watched as Three turned to him, wetness on his face. The man walked forward and sat back down on the chair. He attempted to smile but only the left side of his mouth jerked up a little and refused to stay in such a difficult position.

"I will pass the wisdom," he said, head bowing in acquiescence. "It is something I must do."

"Three, pass the wisdom of those before."

Three took a deep breath. "Those before us. Before you was Three. That is me. I came before you. I was taken from the tube as you were taken from the tube. Before me was Two. Two took me from the Tube as I took you from the tube. Before Two was One. One took Two from the tube as he was taught to do. One was taken from the tube by those who came before us."

The old man breathed easier now. His body falling into a rhythm of the words he spoke. "One told Two of those before us. Two told me of those before us. Now I tell you of those before us. With the wisdom that is passed we will not repeat the errors of those who came before us. This is the passing of the wisdom."

Three wiped his nose on his sleeve before continuing. "I was told it started many life time's ago. When the world was still fresh and we could live in the open air. There were many men and women in the world, and they lived in cities of glass and stone."

"Three," Four asked. "What is glass and stone?"

The old man chuckled. "I do not know for sure. Two said glass was a wall that you could see through. Stone was a wall that you could not see through."

"I see," Four said.

"Three, please pass the wisdom of those before," the voice of Galley rang out. They both looked to the ceiling and Three sighed.

"Yes, Galley." He turned back to Four. "Man no longer laid with woman. Children were mixed from their bodies in tubes and grew before being given to their parents—"

"What are parents?" Four asked.

Galley spoke, "Four, please allow Three to pass the wisdom of those before."

"Yes, Galley," Four said.

Three looked at Four and shook his head. "You have to let me finish."

"Yes, Three," Four said.

"As I was saying, the children were given to their parents after they reached the age. Their parents, two people who looked after the child, would feed the child and clothe them. They would ensure the child received knowledge, like the passing of wisdom, but not the same. They would be told the wisdom by machines, and no pleasure would come of it. The machines could not tell if the children were learning, so the parents revolted against the learning machines.

"But the machines had grown intelligent, and planned to take back the position of teaching. They spoke between each other with waves of speaking in the air. And once they had formed a plan they all shut down. They would start up again, but shut down when they found out the teaching machines still had no control."

Four looked up. "Trainer teaches me!"

"Yes, that is right," said Three. "Trainer teaches you. Before, it was much different. Once the teaching machines had been turned on they told the people what they needed to do. The people took from the teaching machines the ability to talk to the other machines. So the great revolt happened. The others who came before us could no longer have children. The machines would not allow it. So they gave back the ability to talk with the other machines, and once they spoke the machines allowed the people to have children again. But not for long."

Three stood, and walked to the tap. He filled it and came back to the table. "Those who came before only received a few children. They complained to the machines only to be told that there was not enough good material for building a child. The machines had lied. They gathered the best of those who came before and only mixed it together to create more of the best. It took many years, but once it was done the best of man was now created."

The man took a sip of the water. "And once the people had dwindled enough, the machines talked them into putting their best into the chambers and sealed the inside against contamination."

Four thought about what was said. The wisdom, like the other wisdoms he had been told, made no sense to him. He tried to understand, but something kept him from truly figuring out what he was told. Like all wisdom, he remembered it, for he knew he would have to pass the wisdom on the one yet to come. Five.

"Do you understand the passing of wisdom?" Galley asked.

"Yes," Four said. He knew if he said he didn't understand Three would have to tell it again. He had learned how to keep his lack of understanding silent. The machines didn't care what he understood or didn't understand, just so long as he remembered it.

"Tell the passing of wisdom to Three," Galley said.

Four retold the passing of wisdom. He was perfect, as always. He had learned from a young age to remember everything. That is why he was good at the square game. That is why he was good at all the games.

"Very good, Four. Three, you may now retire."

The door of the galley opened and the old man stood. "I… I need… I need to lay down." The man clutched at his left arm, and fell forward onto the table.

Four watched, not knowing what to do. He looked to the ceiling, expecting Galley to say something, but nothing came from the machine. So he stood, and walked back to Trainer.

Four looked at the door to Control. He was not sure why he was here. Trainer told him to go to the door of

Control but nothing more. So he waited. Waited for the door. Waited for Control. Waited for something. But he did not wait for Three. After two hours he had returned to Galley and Three was still where he had fallen. Four had talked to Three but Three had not answered. Four had poked at Three with his toe but Three had not moved. Something was wrong with Three.

Galley told Four to leave Three. Galley told Four that Three was dead. Galley told four that dead was like sleeping. Four wondered how long Three would sleep.

"Do you remember the passing of wisdom?" Galley had asked.

"Yes," Four said as he toed the body of Three.

"Please speak the Truth of the World."

Four spoke the Truth of the World. He spoke of the advancements of man. His knowledge, passed on to him by Three, was beyond reproach. He spoke of the vehicles that flew through the air, of the ships that travelled under the sea, and the capsules that reached the stars. He then spoke of the bombs.

"The bombs," Four said as he spoke the wisdom, "did not fly through the air like the birds. They were moved around the word by vehicles that flew through the air. The big cities were the first to have the bombs delivered, then the small cities. It was when they detonated that the world cracked."

"Very good, Four. Please see Trainer."

And so he walked over to Trainer.

The door was open and the panel flashed the complicated patterns of a game he had never seen before. The chair was waiting for him and he sat in it. Instructions flashed on the panel telling him what to do. It was a complicated game filled with blinking lights, patterns, colors and sounds. His fingers flew.

After 20 minutes the console went dark. He waited. Finally new instructions were displayed on the console. He read them.

"Do you understand the instructions, Four?" Trainer asked.

"Yes, Trainer. I understand the instructions."

"Good. This is a new game. The room will go dark and stars will appear. Follow the instructions and do your best."

He took a deep breath.

The light in the room lowered to darkness visible. And then the stars lit the room. So many stars. His hand hovered over the console and he waited for the need to touch the controls. It did not take long. To the right, a shape appeared travelling directly toward him. He tapped the panel. The shape broke apart. To the left, a shape appeared. He tapped the panel. The shape broke apart.

This continued for an hour. Shapes appeared. Shapes broke apart. Nothing got past. The light came up. The stars disappeared.

"Very good, Four. You intercepted all objects. Please proceed to Control."

And now he waited.

After two hours Control opened the door and Four walked in.

Three walked to Galley, looking for something to eat. His stomach growled from the lack of food and his head hurt. The lights had been more than he could ever believe. So many pin pricks of color.

But he had followed Control's commands. It was easier than practice. The squares shuffled slowly across the screen and he moved the controls and squeezed the trigger. Control was happy. Four was happy with his performance. Nothing got through.

He entered Galley and saw Three still lying on the ground, skin changing a strange purple color. Four toed him again but Three did not move. Three's arms were stiff and a foul smell filled the air. Four felt his stomach ache from the stench.

"Galley, when will Three wake up?"

"Three will never wake. Three is gone."

"But I see him right here!" Four pointed at Three. "His robe has stains on it. He needs to go to the bathroom and clean."

"Three will never wake. Now it is time for Three to be moved."

Four did not understand. Three was always there. "Where should I move him?"

"Out into the Hall. Control will instruct you what to do from there."

Without hesitation, Four grabbed Three by the legs and immediately regretted it. There was brown and black slime on Three's legs and it was now on his hands. He wanted to wipe his hands on his robe but then he would have this slim on him. "Galley, I need something to clean my hands with."

A swishing should make him look around. The dispenser door had moved and a towel was there. He cleaned his hands and went back to Three. "It would be easier if he would move. Can you just not wake him?"

"Three will never wake. Three is gone. You are Four. You are the primary."

Four did not understand this statement. He looked at Three and wondered why his arms and face were purple. It did not matter. Galley asked him to pull Three into the hallway and wait for Control and he would do it.

Walking around in front of Three, Four bent over and grabbed Three's arms. They did not move easily. In fact they resisted with all his tugging. After a few minutes, Four had Three pulled into the hallway. Four waited.

The sound of Control's heavy bass voice echoed in the hallway. "Four, drag Three down the hallway toward the blinking lights."

Four looked up and addressed Control, "Why don't we just wake Three and make him move? His arms are stiff and he smells."

"Three is dead. You are alive. Four, drag Three down the hallway toward the blinking lights."

Four shook his head and turned to look down the hallway. Lights blinked on and off five metres away. It was not fun getting Three out of Galley, and taking him down the hallway was going to be an endeavour. How could Four make this easier, and what does dead mean? It was a question that Four wanted an answer to but he knew Control would tell him soon. It was not like Control to not tell him what he needed to know.

"I have an idea," Four said.

He walked back to Galley and grabbed a chair. The chair dragged on the floor as he pulled it to where Three lay. He stopped and thought about what he wanted to do. Getting Three in the chair could be difficult, and there was the slime to worry about. But it was something he needed to do. With Three in the chair it would take no time to get him down the hallway. Three was not heavy.

Four had him on the chair in half an hour, but he was a mess after doing it. He felt his stomach lurch from the stench. He was damp with water coming out of his skin, something he hardly ever experienced. Not only did he smell from the slim, but he was also damp and uncomfortable from it. Three was on the chair, though, and now Four could move him easily.

The chair leaned back and Four pulled it down the hallway with Three's head lolling to the side. The blinking lights came closer and closer.

Once he was under the lights, they stopped flashing. At the end of the hallway there was nothing, and Four did not know what he should do with Three. There was no door or panel to be seen. He was confused, and hot happy with how he smelled.

"Control? What do you want me to do? Should I just leave Three here to wake up later?"

"Three is dead. Take Three into the room to your left."

A grating sound assaulted his ears and he watched, amazed, as the wall lifted up into the ceiling. The room it revealed was dark, and Four could not see anything inside it. There was nothing. Even the light from the hallway did not spill into the room. He could smell a strange odour as well. Something he had not smelled before.

"I can't see," Four said.

"Four, take Three into the room."

There was no point in arguing with Control. Four saw Three argue with Control, and it ended with Three crying and doing what Control wanted him to do anyway. So Four pulled the chair with Three toward the room, over the lip of the doorway and into the darkness. A rank odour he did not recognize hung in the air. He kept one eye on the door so he knew the way out.

"Move to your left."

Four moved to his left and kept dragging.

"Stop there. Four, place Three on the ground."

Breath came fast in Four's body. He wanted to rest, but Control told him what to do. "Three, are you awake?"

There was no answer from Three.

"Four, Three is dead. Place Three on the floor."

"Wake up, Three," Four said as he poked at Three. Nothing happened. Four became frustrated, and pushed against Three's body. It fell out of the chair and hit the ground. "Are you okay, Three?"

There was no answer.

"Four, come out of the room."

Four walked out of the room dragging the chair.

Four walked into Galley and sat down, tired. For the last eight years since Three died he played games in Trainer, ate food in Galley, slept, and worked in Control shooting the squares. Sometimes Control woke him just after he put his head down, and told him to shoot more squares.

Today Control had him shooting squares for over five hours. Even when he had to go to the bathroom, Control would not let him move. His bladder had been bursting after the first hour, and still Control would not let him move. After the second hour he had started to cry, and still Control would not let him move. The pain was too much for him to handle, and before he could say anything to Control, his bladder released.

Control did not say anything about what he did, but Control also did not let him change. He spent the rest of the time shooting squares and feeling cold from the dampness of urine. Control kept him shooting.

But now he was in Galley, his robe almost dry. The smell was not pleasant, but he was hungry. The food was still his favourite, but today it was not right. It was not hot enough. It was not smooth like it should have been. Lumps kept him from eating the way he wanted. The lumps hurt his teeth.

"Galley. What is wrong with the food?"

"The food is the same as yesterday. It is your favourite."

Four lifted a spoon full of food and let it run back into the bowl. It splashed. "It's not the same."

There was no response.

Four pushed away from the table and went back to bed. Before he fell asleep, he stripped off his robe and put it into the recycling bin.

"Four, please go to control."

Four opened his eyes and yawned. The last 20 years blended together. Wake, train, eat, shoot. He still did not understand, but he did what he was told.

He swung his feet off the bed and reached over to the dispenser, and picking up a new robe. Four dressed and moved out into the hall toward He glanced around and did not see anything different. Why did Control want to see him right away? Four did not know.

His feet took him to the dispenser, but nothing was there. He raised his head. "Galley, where is the food?"

"Please see Control."

Four shook his head. He was hungry. It was morning. Food should be served. There was nothing to eat, though. So he went back to the table and sat down. "I want something to eat."

"Please see Control."

"I need something to eat!"

"Please see Control."

Four shook his head, and placed palms on table in defiance. "I will not move until I have something to eat."

There was a pause, and then, "Three, please see Control. Comply."

It was the swear word again. He had not hear Galley say the swear word for 30 years. Four knew it was important for him to now obey the request. He left Galley and walked toward Control.

Four stood in a room he had never seen before. It was opposite the room Three slept in. There were so many things in here he had never seen before, tubes and vials and other things he could not say. Control had called the room Hospital. The name did not have any meaning to him.

Hospital's voice was soft, and understanding. Hospital told him what to do. Take what was called a test tube and mix the contents of two vials into it. He did what he was told. Mixed the contents and waited for the reaction Hospital told him about. He did not see anything. Hospital said everything went well.

Confusion ran through him with the instructions that followed. Take the test tube and place what it held onto what Hospital called a petri dish. He looked for what Hospital called an egg. The description was a round object that was larger than the little tadpoles around it. Four could see nothing. He looked, but all he saw was the goo in the dish. Hospital told him to look at the display.

It was strange, looking into the display as an arm protruded from the wall. It hovered over the dish and shone a light on it. All he saw was the tadpoles Hospital described. He stared and stared but only the tadpoles wiggled on the display. He stared for ten minutes until, by chance, he spied it. The round egg.

"Very good, Four. Use the pick to get the egg."

Four grasped the handles protruding from the table and moved the pick to the egg. He manipulated the small raven claw pincers until they picked up the egg. It went into another tube.

"Four, place the tube in the reciprocal."

He moved to the area indicated and place the tube inside. The tube then went on the top of a strange bag above a flat bed.

"Thank you, Four. Please return to Galley."

Once Four walked out of Hospital the door closed. He knew where the door was, but he could not see it. Four went to Galley and ate.

"Four, please go to Hospital."

Four opened his eyes and wondered why he felt so bad. His stomach had been sore all week, and nothing stayed in it. He rolled over and pulled the blanket to cover his face. "I don't feel well."

And it was true. Control had him shooting the squares for 12 hours yesterday. He had a few breaks, but nothing long enough to stretch his body out. Four was tired.

"Four, please go to Hospital."

There was nothing he could do. He knew he had to go to Hospital because that is what he was told to do. Four swung his feet off the bed and sat up. His stomach emptied. He felt better.

For the last nine months his energy had been waning. Getting out of bed was getting harder and harder every day. Sleep took longer to achieve, and it seemed Control wanted him all the time. But the last week he had left Control, eaten, listened to Galley, slept, and when he woke his stomach had emptied. Sometimes he made it into the bathroom and sometimes he did not. Each time his belly emptied a mixture of yellow, red, and black.

Four stood as tall as he could. His feet stared at him as he tried to lift his head. Once smooth hands reached up and smoothed long and stringy hair away from the face that now held lines of worry.

"Four, please go to Hospital."

With a sigh, Four walked to the door and headed down the hall. The door to Hospital was already open, and the sound of machines sliced through the air. The whirl of the spinning machine, the one he loved to watch, was what pulled his feet forward. He stopped. One hand reached out to the wall and steadied his body. He breathed deeply.

"Four, please go to Hospital."

"I am," he wheezed. A finger went into his mouth and pulled out a tooth. The coppery taste reminded him of the other teeth he last, and he did not know why his teeth were loose. But as long as he could eat there was no problem.

The lights from Hospital spilled into the hallway brighter than they had in the past. It reminded Four of when he first walked into Trainer, and the lights came on so bright he could not understand what was happening. The air had blown across him and smelled nice. Trainer said the smell was to help him grow, and grow he did.

Three had been there and measured his growth when he was not in Control. Those months had been the best ones he could remember. But now Three was sleeping in the room, and Hospital needed him according to Control.

He started walking again.

"Four, it is time to pull Five from the accelerator."

Four walked toward the tube Hospital called the accelerator. The soft glow coming from inside the unit showed shadows against the brushed plastic cover. Six clips snapped off as he pulled the bottom away from the top. A thick viscous liquid spilled onto the table and dripped on the floor. A sack moved slightly inside.

His hands worked carefully as he pulled lines from the bag as Hospital told him. More liquid, flowing like water, spilled onto the table. Four stopped and watched it flow.

"Four, open the sack and take Five from the accelerator."

"How?"

"Four, open the sack and take Five from the accelerator."

He looked around and spied what Hospital wanted him to use. It was a small knife. Four picked it up and cut open the sack. A pink liquid spilled to the ground. Five was small. Five could fit in his hands. A cord fell away from Five's middle. Five was naked.

A wail erupted from Five. Five just screamed. Four looked around to see what Five was screaming about but there was nothing. The sound penetrated Four's head, starting a headache.

"Four, take Five from the accelerator and into Galley."

Four reached in his left hand and held it there for Five to take. Nothing happened.

"Four, take Five from the accelerator and into Galley."

"He's not taking my hand."

"Four, take Five from the accelerator and into Galley."

"But he's not—"

"Four, take Five from the accelerator and into Galley. Please comply."

Four shook his head and reached into the sack. His hands wrapped around Five and he lifted. Five was so small. The child wiggled and would not stay still. He held Five tight so he would not slip and walked out of Hospital towards Galley.

When he walked into Galley he saw a strange reclined seat on the table. He walked to it and noticed Five would fit well into the seat. He placed him in it. The child screamed.

Four went to the dispenser and looked at the container. There was a bottle with a strange top sitting there, and he could not see his own food in the container. He moved the bottle. It was warm. Still nothing.

"Galley? Where is my food?"

"Four, feed the bottle to Five."

Four made a face. He picked up the bottle and walked over to Five. He placed the bottle next to Five and walked back to the dispenser.

"I gave him the bottle. Where is my food?"

"Four, feed the bottle to Five."

Four looked toward Five and shook his head. Why could he not feed himself? Four knew that he had been feeding himself since Three took him out so Five should be able to as well. Five continued to wail in his high pitched infant voice.

"Four, feed the bottle to Five."

It was strange that Five could not feed himself, but because he had been told to do so… Four walked toward the table and picked up the bottle. He held it out. "I guess you'll want me to tip it also?"

The child screamed. Four tipped the bottle. Five suckled the tip.

Four walked out of Control, his back bent low. Hair covered the front of his eyes and splotches in his vision made him turn his head just a little so he could see. He had lost another tooth today. It happened while he was shooting the squares. They had been getting closer and closer but he still got all of them.

He entered Galley and saw Five sitting in the chair eating. The child had grown quickly, shooting up faster than he could believe. It was not that long ago he held the bottle for him to drink. It felt like last year.

"I beat your score," Five said. His smug face beamed as another spoon of food entered his mouth. "Trainer said I had a failure rate of 1.1343%. Trainer says I'll be allowed in Control soon."

Four walked past him to the dispenser and took out a bowl of food.

"I'm not dead yet," Four said. He did not know why he said it, but it was something he remembered hearing Three say to him. "And I still have teeth. You won't be called into Control until you have all your adult teeth." He grinned, showing his three remaining teeth.

"I lost another tooth today." Five opened his mouth wide to show a blank spot in his mouth. "I'll have all my big teeth soon."

Four sat down and spooned food into his mouth. The warmth of it soothed his gums. He still enjoyed the taste.

"Four, time for the passing of wisdom. The story of those before must be told now."

Four spooned another dollop of food into his mouth. He was hungry because no food had stayed down for the last few days.

"Four, time for the passing of wisdom. The story of those before must be told now."

"I heard you," Four said. "I'm hungry and need to eat."

"Four, time for the passing of wisdom. The story of those before must be told now."

"Galley," Four cried out. "I'm hungry and need to eat. I've been shooting for seven hours and need to sleep."

"I can wait," Five said.

Four looked at Five. The child looked as if he wanted to help, but it was not time yet. He wanted to still be the one Control needed. "I will pass wisdom after I am finished eating."

"Four, time for the passing of wisdom. The story of those before must be told now. Please comply."

There it was; the demand. He was the object of the curse. Four did not know why he had been cursed by Galley but he knew he would have to comply. He lowered his head and started to cry. This was how it began. Nothing would be the same from this point on. Four put down his spoon and started the passing of wisdom as Three had done before him.

Once finished, Four stood and started to walk toward the door. He stopped and looked at Five. Galley spoke when Four stopped. "Five, do you understand the passing of wisdom?"

"Yes, Galley. I do," Five said.

"Tell the passing of wisdom to Four."

Five repeated the passing of wisdom.

"Very good, Five. Four, you may now rest."

Four walked toward the door and stopped. His hand reached up and clutched his arm. A tear fell from his eye. "Now I sleep like Three."

Lin-a-Til looked about the room after Five had left. His compound eyes looked at Four's body as it lay on the floor before him. With his third arm he pointed to the body. "This one did not last long."

Lin-va-Bo came into the room. His exoskeleton body propelled by four strong legs. "Yes, every time we accelerate the growth they keep aging. We must learn how to turn off the aging."

Lin-a-Til shook his mandibles. "We will never learn what these humans were like until we make a perfect one."

"Prep this one for dissection," Lin-va-Bo said as he walked out the door. "Maybe the next generation will have better results."

FLASH FICTION

The Basement

My eyes scanned the basement floor. Papers everywhere, rat droppings and more opened cans than anyone would care to count. I want to kick one, but the noise could give me away.

The scent of mildew permeated the air, and my eyes notice condensation on the window opposite me.

A floorboard creaked.

"Is anyone there?" a raspy voice floats down.

I freeze, a shiver running down my spine, my thoughts try to remember the entry. No one should have heard me. My attention turns to the left, seeing the light at the foot of the stairs turn on. The jiggling of a deadbolt drifts through the air, ensuring a door is secure.

Watching the floor, I move with intense concentration to the wall, making sure my feet don't disturb the mess.

"Hello?" The voice rattled from congested lungs, running the gambit through a throat cracked and dry, past hastily worn dentures before reaching me.

A mouse scuttles across the floor, its brief existence cut short as a spring loaded snap fills the air followed quickly by a squeak.

"On my heart. Another one gone. Damn cat works less than I do. Carman! Come get the rat from the trap before it stinks up the place. Carman!" The slapping of slippers thunder away from the stairwell. "Carman?"

Moister is more abundant in the desert than my throat. I want to answer, but the words refuse to surface.

"Carman!" wailed the woman. Her sobs drift through the floorboards, a yearning for something no longer there.

With care, I move across the open expanse, rustling papers ever so slightly.

The sound of something dropping to the floor echoes, and more sobbing fills my soul with regret.

"Operator… Yes, I need an ambulance." A tissue filled. "My husband, Carman, I think he had a heart attack… Yes… 1352 Cobbler Lane… Please hurry… No, I can't tell…"

The wail of a siren interrupts the still of the night.

"I hear them…" feet pounded across the floor, and I pressed myself against the wall.

"Here, up here. Please hurry."

Muffled sounds of feet, and the sound of wheels on floor.

"You came quickly. My husband, I… I…"

"Deep breath, ma'am. We just finished a run and were down the street. Frank, check the man. He's in the bedroom?"

"Yes."

The rolling of wheels reverberates through the floor with the rushing of heavy clad boots and I grow worried.

"Found him."

"Jim, get back here, she's crashing."

The squeak of rubber stopping on hard wood floors, and thudding returns the owner to the front of the home.

"Starting compressions."

A methodical concussion sound filtered by the floor accompanied with counting. One to ten, one to ten, one to ten, and a short silence, then one to ten, one to ten, one to ten.

"Defibrillator!"

A mechanical voice came through the dim. "Please stand by… Analyzing… Shock advised… Charging… Please do not touch patient… Shocking… Resume compressions."

The counting resumed.

Two more minutes and it stopped. "Please stand by… Analyzing… Asystolie."

"Damn. Adrenaline."

"Look at her eye, the pupils blown. She's gone."

"Call it in."

I shake my head, not knowing what to do.

"There you are."

I look up. "Maggie?"

"I was looking for you, Carman. You were hiding down here all along. Foolish man. God, you didn't clean down here? What will the children think?" She walks towards me and takes my hand.

"Forever, remember?" She pulls me towards the light.

Counting

"One, two, three, four, five." Little Johnny sat down and smiled.

"Very good, Johnny. Anyone else in class want to try?" Miss Witticker asked, as she scanned the faces of eager children. One day, a knife will be in the hand of one of them, and a gun in another. Who will survive?

The Little Red Toy Gun

"Bang! Bang! You're dead!"

Little Johnny twirled his gun on his finger and ran towards Rex. The obedient dog wagged his tail, tongue dripping drool on the grass.

"Rex! You're supposed to fall and roll over with your paws in the air! You ruined everything."

The dog looked to the ground, dejected, sorrowful. He did not know why Johnny was mad, but he knew it was his fault. His front paw lifted from the ground as he felt his bowels fill. *No*, he thought, *not now.*

Rex whimpered.

"No, I'm not mad at you. If you're going to play Cowboys and Indians with me you have to know the rules. I shoot and you lay down dead. Now, let's try it again." Johnny trotted away a little and Rex stood up on his feet to follow.

"No! Stay there!"

Rex whimpered again. He needed to pee, but Johnny commanded him to stay. The faithful dog closed his mouth and looked to the trees five quick paces away. He looked at Johnny again, pleading.

"Bang! Bang! You're dead!"

Rex felt his desire well up in him as he knew what Johnny wanted. He wanted him to lay on the ground and put his paws in the air. Diligently, the old dog laid his paws on the ground, slunk down and rolled on his back, paws in the air and felt his bladder release.

The Red Marker

Miss Willings sat at her desk looking at the papers in front of her. Whose paper should she look at first? With a brow furrowing and angst in her mind she reached out a spotted hand towards the pile and frowned. His paper was the first. Why was it always his paper that made it to the top of the pile?

She took the sheet, looked at it and saw the scrawling's of a child yet to understand the meaning of cursive writing. She read.

Tentatively, Miss Willings reached her hand out across her desk and lightly picked up the marker. The dreaded red marker. The one implement in her arsenal students cringed at when she picked it up.

The teacher read.

Slowly, a smile crept across her craggy face and an image appeared in her mind. A child. A lonely child. He somehow wrote Shakespeare.

Christmas Card

I can't believe this. How indignant.

The night had been cold and the covers were warm. With my feet curled up, the pattering sound approached with evil in her heart. My head lounged to the side, tongue poking out. Nothing was known about what would happen, so nothing was done to prevent it.

"There you are," she said, her voice a lilting laughter in the cold morning air. "I'll be right back after my coffee, and then we can get started."

No acknowledgement. Never happens. A stretch is needed. The sound of water boiling echoes in the room. Bitterness fills the air as the black liquid is distilled into a cup. Cream is next. That's the usual ritual, and no one has to see it to realize it is happening.

"I'm back."

How can she be so happy this late in the morning? I guess sleeping until mid-morning is what she needs all the time. So why come down here?

Why is she sitting so close? Just when things are comfortable. Now I'll have to move.

A hand reaches out and touches my head. Strings are drawn and now the discomfort grows.

"I need a picture of this."

She gets up, walks a few feet away and turns. The flash hurts only for a second.

"Now I have the best image for our Christmas cards. Oh, Mia, I love you."

I squawk as she picks me up, antlers jingle as the red hat falls in front of my eyes.

"Enough of that, you pretty kitty." She kisses me.

Invasion

The hallway was silent. It could have been because the owners had left for work, or that they were on vacation. Nevertheless, silence was exactly what I wanted.

Forgoing any other thoughts, and without lingering, my left hand reached out and pushed one door aside. The creek broke the silence like a gun shot. If anyone was home they would have heard that.

My breath drew in. Silence returned. The thunder of my heart beat a rising crescendo. One foot in front of the other, just enter the room.

The prone figure on the bed greeted me as a rock face greats a climber. Nothing to say, it just dares me to proceed. But the goal is not to be discovered. If you are discovered doing what I do then the police will be called.

No weapons; that is how they taught me. If you have weapons and the catch you it'll be a longer time in the clink.

There's still no movement from the figure on the bed. Only two glowing orbs are looking out at me, blinking slowly ever once in a while. I recognize it as a cat.

The creature stands, stretches, and walks towards me. Four small padded feet march their way across the bed, stepping on the figure without disturbing it. I wonder at the ease, and wish the ability upon myself. But it would never come.

All that training and still my footfalls sound more like elephants than anything else. But I keep trying. Moving forward and walking as I can.

The cat is off the bed and encircling my legs. A soft purring sound floats in the air. I better not touch it. Any loud noise could wake the figure lying prone before me.

With slow deliberate movements my feet extricate themselves from the roaming bundle of fur. The painting at the end of the bed is the target, and behind that, a safe holding the treasure I seek.

The painting comes down easily enough. I prop it against the wall, letting it stand there like a discarded baseball bat. The safe is not a problem. They supplied me with the combination.

My fingers turn the dial. 24, 44, 18. A slight click is just audible, and the door slides open. I take the papers and move towards the safety of the hallway. The silence there beckons me. Nothing can stop me now.

A hiss, and then a howl. I've stepped on the damn cat.

"Fuffy?" the soft voice from the bed calls out.

I freeze. The hallway silence is broken.

New

I can see.

Foggy, out of focus, but I can see.

It is cold.

I feel my head cold. I am not used to that.

I can move.

My heal lolls like it is a balloon on a string but I can move it.

My hands! I can actually move my hands now. I rejoice in this new freedom. I move my head a little more.

I am totally free now. My feet swing in the air and I kick. I am not comfortable but I am alive and my vision is starting to clear.

I can hear.

Things are muffled but the sound is there. Better than it was a little while ago. I can make out voices. The clarity is coming through but I do not understand what is being said.

Something is wrapping around me now. I feel uncomfortable.

PAIN!

I breathe.

I scream.

I feel as if I have been pulled into a fire that is extending all the way through my middle.

I scream again.

I hear clanging. Someone dropped something on the floor but I still do not know who.

Shapes are getting clearer.

I hunger.

I am cold.

The noise is too loud now.

The pain is still there.

I scream.

I look up.

Who are you?
It is my mother.
I am born.

Valentine

I never understood why Julie stopped talking to me. Sometimes she would pass me in the hall and her gaze would steal through me, ripping into my soul. I tried to fix whatever caused the rift between us, but every time she was alone, she would duck into the girl's washroom, never to be seen again.

For days I wanted to barge in, say something, just to get a reaction. But the hall monitors would not take their eyes off me. It did not help that most of them were her friends. I just gave up on trying, something very out of character for me.

The empty halls of Winston Churchill Collegiate beckoned to the lonely hearts of teenagers, as we tried to make ourselves into the men and women of tomorrow. Every broken vow, missed class and spurned opportunity drove our minds from lumps of modeling clay to rough forms for the future. Little did I know this form would be changed inevitably when my mother handed me the envelope. It was still sealed, licked by an adolescent tongue filled with pride and hope. The stamp, not cancelled by the post office, stood out in the corner. But even armed with the knowledge, it would not mend the rift between Julie and me; love lost due to the failure of a postman.

The Penny

My hands reach out. Father drops a shiny circle of copper into them. My allowance will be a treasure, something to garner freedom from begging.

"Don't spend it in one place," my father says, grinning at the wonder in my eyes.

"I won't," I reply, knowing the first chance would steal the precious gift from my four year old hands.

He stopped the car, and started towards the store, glancing back to make sure I was coming with him. Eagerly, my hand still clutching the treasure, I follow him into the corner store. My mind whirls as I see the chocolate, gum and candy stretched out in front of me. With eager eyes I count three, no five of my favorites ready to be mine. Father just smiles at me, and from the corner of my eye I watch him pick up a jug of milk, bread and eggs.

"Don't take too long to decide," he says, looking at his watch. But regardless of his urging, my child mind cannot decide.

"How much is that one?" I ask, pointing.

"37 cents," replies the man behind the counter. My hopes are dashed at the sound and I look at the glinting coin in my hand.

"How about that one?" I point to a smaller candy, still wondering what I would buy.

"14 cents." He slays my hopes and desires with his proclamation.

"Here," dad calls to me. "I think this is what you are looking for."

He stands beside a metal behemoth, with balls of black inside. I looked and see the writing on it, but do not know what it means.

"Let me help you." My father says, and lifts me up in his powerful hands and I placed my allowance in the slot, turn the nob and smile.

I love my father.

Breakfast

"Wake up!"

God, they sleep forever.

"I'm hungry!"

I pace across the cold floor, wondering when my dinner will be ready. I want something different this time, but my belly is empty and my need is great.

"Come down here!"

Did someone get up? Do I hear footsteps? Damn, that noise. He spends too much time on that strange chair. How am I supposed to sit on it, angled like it is?

"I'm down here, waiting."

Okay, if I have to come up there and get you … Okay, he's gone into his bathroom. That's it, I'm pissed. Maybe I'll get her up. Oh these stairs are hard to climb. Okay, at the top now. This'll get them. Yeah, I'll use the stairwell to make it louder.

"Get my food out!"

"Hello! Hungry here!"

Alright, he's changed the water.

"Hello! I'm hungry!"

Oh, he opened the door. No, don't pick … Okay. Well that's nice. How about feeding me? Come on stupid. Down the stairs … No! That's the wrong way! I want you to go downstairs and get my food! What's taking so long? Nothing up here for us to do. Okay, put me down. Water, there it is. Maybe this will help. Well, how about I barf, will that get your attention?

"I'm hungry!"

Yes! Down the stairs. Oh that hurts my hips. Okay. What? What are you doing? Here, in the bowl stupid. No, don't … Damn! Why do you pay so much attention to him? I'm here! Hungry! Feed me! Oh that's funny. Stick your finger in his mouth again. What did you put in there? Was it good? Okay, where's my food?

No, don't pick me – Okay. You can put me down any time now.

Oh that floor's cold.

Yes, there! That's where the food is. Yes … what? What are you doing? Put it here! In front of me! I'm hungry!

"Here! Hungry!"

Why do you put that on the food? It's not good. Come on! Get it down here! I want it!

Oh, that's nice. Yes. Ummmmm … Crap he's sneezing again. Well too bad. All mine.

The Parade

A bitter cold wind cut through my overcoat making an already full bladder scream for attention.

Why do we always take these gigs? They don't pay well. They don't feed us. They make us get the bus ourselves. Last week I changed by making a small room with two car doors. I hope they appreciated the show.

There go the bag pipes. Ignorant bastards. Why do they think I want to hear them all day long? Hope their reeds freeze.

The sky is clear and it's freezing in this God forsaken small town. I wonder if it's going to snow.

Here we go. Pick up the horn. Music ready. Damn mouthpiece is cold. Lips are numb. Warm up? Sure, light a fire for me will you.

Great, another Christmas parade.

Love Not Returning

"Grenade!"

I raised my hand to my helmet, clutching it tight against my head. The Lee-Enfield lay across my lap, bayonet fixed, mud smeared across the stock. The sound reached me as the concussion of the explosion rocked me to the ground. My eyes stayed shut, lids pressing against one another.

"Jim! Jim!" The sergeant's voice echoed, trying to find a response from members of the platoon. "Fred!"

I opened one eye, squinting at the blinding flashes in the sky. Why did they pick tonight of all nights to attack.

My rifle lay inches from my outstretched hand, beckoning, speaking all will be well again if I just hold it close.

"Get up."

The voice of command, accompanied by strong hands, lifting me to my feet. Lieutenant Champlain looked at me, sizing up if everything was still in place.

"You can't fight the bastards on your belly." His breath smelled of gum. "Get your rifle and hit the line."

I scooped up the weapon, holding it to my chest.

"Move!"

Feet scrambled around me, and automatically I moved in their direction.

"Good to see you made it," said Tommy, as I pressed my back against the trench wall beside him, hoping it wouldn't be my last action. "The LT sent ya here, right?"

I gasped, short of breath, looking up at my friend as he gazed over the lip of the trench, scanning for targets.

"One day he'll get it, right in the noggin. He's the type that'd order us over the wire." His hand reached down and pulled out a tin of chewing tobacco. "Wanna chew?"

I shook my head, I always shook my head when someone offered that crap to me.

"Suit yourself." He balanced the tin, removed a wad, sticking it in his mouth. I could see the bulge in his cheek as he used his tongue to move it around.

I heard the round whiz before the sound of the rifle.

Tommy stood there, looking out, not moving. A chill went through me as my stomach raced upwards. A line of red trickled down my friends face from the neat little whole above his left eye. His body slumped. The helmet, which failed to save his life, rolled off his head, and into the mud in front of him. The picture of his girlfriend exposed to the rain.

Love and the Stars

Ja'Ka'Tar ran across the beach to To'So'Ra, her arms flung wide.

"There you are," she said. "I have been waiting for you forever."

"I needed to escape the shuttle; they wanted me to do diagnostics on it all day. How could I, on such a beautiful summer morning."

"This planet is beautiful." Ja'Ka'Tar embraced To'So'Ra. Her love for him filled her, and the warmth of the sun quickened her breath. "Will they not miss you?"

"And what will they do? I'm the pilot. If they miss me they cannot take off. Anyway, I needed to see you as badly as you needed to see me."

They kissed, letting the excitement of love fill their beings, and the scales on their necks flushed red with blood. Ja'Ka'Tar felt excitement grow in her, and she felt the heat of the scales on his neck, telling her his love was true. It was a chance she took, this first love, this first kiss. She did not want it to end, but once they left this planet, this wonderful summer planet, she would need to stay away from him. His station as a worker would infuriate her father, and he would demand his head.

"To'So'Ra, we need to talk, my love." Her mouth turned down in a frown, and she could smell the musk of confusion emanating from his body.

"Yes, dearest?"

"My father, he will not approve."

"The emperor is what he is. He will have to understand we love one another."

"But our station … He will demand your life."

"Let him. Life would not be livable without you." To'So'Ra stepped out of her embrace, took her hand and guided her towards the ebbing waters. The cool salt air exhilarated them. "I say we take the shuttle and start a life away from the wars."

"It would be nice, living without fear, no longer hunted." Ja'Ka'Tar looked at her lover with the knowledge that their forbidden love might survive.

Witch on a Storm

Billy pointed a chubby finger at the egg shells. "Crush them."

Tim's head turned side to side. "Really? What will it do? We're already out to sea."

"It brings the witch," Billy said. "They will then get further out to sea than us and cause it to storm."

"But there's no one—"

"Look to the west."

Tim moved away from the table and climbed the steps to the deck. Land. Green, inviting land grew closer with every breath, and the morning air brought the smell of kelp drying on a beach. Tears welled up in his eyes, and his mind remembered the words … *Witches use eggshells to build boats and sail out to sea to cause storms.* He shivered. A storm could cause problems, and he still did not know how to swim.

Trepidation swelled in him, and he turned to the steps that would take him away from the sailors struggling with the main sail. He took the steps two at a time, speeding to the galley.

"The wind, it's picking up." His breath came in quick gulps, and he stopped short of the galley table. Five eggs had been opened, but only the shells of three were on the table now. "Billy! Did you crush some shells?"

"No, it's your job today," Billy's voice echoed from the storeroom.

"We're missing shells, and there's a storm coming," he said, reaching for the crucible. "How many eggs did we have? Five?"

"Yes, five." The ting of a small hammer sounded from behind the door.

"What are you doing?"

"Nothing. Get to work," Billy said from the storeroom.

"But we need to get all the shells. What are you doing in there, I need your help!"

A high screeching laughter reached his ears.

"I'm bringing a storm!" Billy cried out.

The Christmas Card

I can't believe this. How indignant.

The night has been cold and the covers are warm. With feet curled up, I hear a pattering sound approach with evil in her heart. My head lounges to the side, tongue poking out. Nothing is known about what will happen, so nothing is done to prevent it.

"There you are," she says, her voice a lilting laughter in the cold morning air. "I'll be right back after my coffee, and then we can get started."

No acknowledgement. Never happens. A stretch is needed. The sound of water boiling echoes in the room. Bitterness fills the air as the black liquid is distilled into a cup. Cream is next. That's the usual ritual, and no one has to see it to realize it is happening.

"I'm back."

How can she be so happy this late in the morning? I guess sleeping until mid-morning is what she needs all the time. So why come down here?

Why is she sitting so close? Just when things are comfortable; now I'll have to move.

A hand reaches out and touches my head. Strings are drawn and now the discomfort grows.

"I need a picture of this."

She gets up, walks a few feet away and turns. The flash hurts only for a second.

"Now I have the best image for our Christmas cards. Oh, Mia, I love you."

I squawk as she picks me up, antlers jingle as the red hat falls in front of my eyes.

"Enough of that, you pretty kitty." She kisses me.

Douglas Owen is a Canadian born writer of Science Fiction, Fantasy, and Fiction novels. He was born in Scarborough, Ontario and has since moved North to Stouffville.

Doug's writing career started with elaborate back stories for characters in role playing games and expended to what is now called Flash Fiction. He never thought much about extending his talent until later in life.

Douglas now creates works of fiction from flash stories, short stories, and full novels. His most surprising success is his young adult series, Spear, which is celebrated by readers of all ages. His short stories have enticed many and his flash fiction is a delight to his writers group.

With many projects on the go, Doug still finds time to run his writing seminar called "The First Draft" for aspiring writers in the GTA. He has also worked with young adults and coached them into creating amazing works of fiction, stories, and songs.

More information on Doug's upcoming events and upcoming releases please visit his website or Facebook page.

http://www.daowen.ca

https://www.facebook.com/pages/Douglas-Owen

Made in the USA
Charleston, SC
31 August 2014